COMANCHE CONFLICT

STONECROFT SAGA 14

B.N. RUNDELL

WOLFPACK PUBLISHING
— EST 2013 —

WOLFPACK
PUBLISHING
— EST 2013 —

Comanche Conflict

Paperback Edition
Copyright © 2021 B.N. Rundell

Wolfpack Publishing
6032 Wheat Penny Avenue
Las Vegas, NV 89122

wolfpackpublishing.com

All rights reserved. No part of this book may be reproduced
by any means without the prior written consent of the
publisher, other than brief quotes for reviews.

This book is a work of fiction. Any references to historical
events, real people or real places are used fictitiously. Other
names, characters, places and events are products of the
author's imagination, and any resemblance to actual events,
places or persons, living or dead, is entirely coincidental.

Paperback ISBN 978-1-64734-997-4
eBook ISBN 978-1-64734-996-7

COMANCHE CONFLICT

DEDICATION

Every day is a precious gift from God and even in this year, (2020) we have learned to appreciate the gift of time. To share even a moment of that precious commodity is a gift from one to another, and I am continuously honored whenever anyone takes those moments to read one of my works. The Bible says we are given "threescore and ten" or seventy years, and if by His grace it is more, then those extra moments are to be savored. I passed the "threescore and ten" mark several years ago, and I have come to appreciate every moment as a precious gift from our Lord and Saviour, moments to be used, appreciated, and shared. And so I share my moments with you, dear reader, as you share yours with me. Thank you.

1 / HUNT

The massive bull bison blew snot, shook his head, and glared with fiery eyes at the man before him. Digging his front hooves deep in the dirt and clawing it back, tossing muddy clods behind him, the bull snorted and charged, his head down and black horns leading the charge. The frantic man, struggling to reload his Lancaster flintlock rifle, looked at the charging beast with wide eyes that showed fear, but he could not move, his horse had fallen, trapping his leg underneath and Ezra kicked and pulled, as he fought with his rifle.

The dusty thick mat of the bull's big head smashed into the shoulder of Ezra, the horns snagging his buckskins, and the impact of the almost two ton beast jerked Ezra's leg free, but the bull bellowed and lifted his head and tossed Ezra tumbling in the air over his back. An arrow drove into the thick brown chest and the bull stumbled over the downed horse, fell to his shoulder, and scrambled back to his feet, turning, and searching for his adversary. Another arrow whispered and skewered the massive beast in the base of his neck, but the great buffalo shook his head and looked for his new target.

Gabe was astride his big black Andalusian stallion, Ebony, guiding him with his knees as he nocked another arrow. The stallion and bull stood forty yards apart, both snorting steam and snot, staring at one another with the challenge of the ancients. Ebony reared high, pawing the sky with his hooves as Gabe grasped a handful of mane to keep his seat. When the stallion's hooves hit the ground, he lunged forward, charging the monstrous master of the plains who lowered his head and leapt into his charge. The ground thundered with the anticipated clash but the rider aboard the stallion, urged his mount to a quick slash to the side, allowing the bull space to pass. The big beast could not maneuver as quickly or adroitly as the stallion and the bull, with head lowered, anticipating the contact, the stallion easily sidestepped, and Gabe let fly the arrow that drove into the lower chest of the beast, burying itself to the fletching.

With the feathers of five arrows fluttering in the breeze, the huge bull appeared as if decorated for battle, but he stumbled, blood dripping from his mouth and spraying from his nose. He staggered like a drunk, trying to focus on the ground before him, stumbled again, and turned for another charge. He snorted, bellowed, and shook his massive head, bloodshot eyes barely showing through the thick fur and dust. He took a step forward, paused and bellowed again. Reaching out one hoof to dig at the dirt and claw it back in the challenge of the flatlands, the bull dripped blood and was too weak to draw back. He shook his head malevolently, gurgled another bellow, leaned into his charge, then fell on his neck, and rolled to the side, his legs extended and twitching, then stilled.

Gabe watched the beast for but a moment, then dug his heels to Ebony to go to his friend, who lay unmoving and contorted in the dirt. Gabe slid to the ground and knelt beside Ezra, saw his chest rise and fall, but his breathing was ragged, and his eyes were but slits. Gabe gently rolled him to his back, began checking for injuries, but was pushed aside when Grey Dove and Cougar Woman came beside him.

Grey Dove, Ezra's Shoshone wife and mother of his two children, touched her man's face, "Ezra, Ezra," she pleaded, but received no response. She looked at Cougar, nodded for her to check Ezra for injuries. Gabe stepped back, knowing the women were more adept than he at this sort of thing, but he knew his friend was badly injured.

"Looks like his leg's broken, and I think he's got some busted ribs," suggested Gabe, dropping to one knee beside his friend. He helped his wife, Cougar

Woman, as she examined Ezra, noting the many abrasions and the ripped tunic that exposed a jagged tear in his shoulder. Gabe pointed, "That's where the bull's horn caught him, looks bad."

Cougar nodded, dug in her parfleche and brought out a folded piece of cloth to wipe at the wound, looked at Gabe, "You wash this," nodding to his water bag on his saddle, "I will make a poultice."

Gabe quickly retrieved the bag, rinsed off the wound and patted it dry, held it down to stem the bleeding until Cougar readied the poultice. She used some water, mixed up her remedy and made the poultice, and with a nod to Gabe to move, she applied it to the wound. After binding it tight with a wide strip of buckskin, she looked at his leg. With a glance to Gabe, "We need four sticks for a splint," nodding toward the nearby stream bordered by willows. Gabe grinned, stood and went to the stream to fetch the needed withes.

When Ezra's big bay horse had dropped his hoof into the prairie dog hole, they both went down, and at that time the bull Ezra had shot, was still on his feet and on the prod. Gabe walked to the big bay, now standing, head down and favoring the left front leg. With a quick examination, Gabe was relieved to see the leg was not broken, but the foreleg was scraped and bleeding, the knee swollen, and the animal would need some attention, but Ezra was the priority. Gabe stroked the neck of the bay, speaking to him and let the rein drop to ground tie the bay and with a whistle called Ebony to his side. The horses had been friends as long as Gabe and Ezra and they understood one another as was obvious when Ebony came to his side, and Gabe reached out to stroke the black's neck and spoke to him. Dropping the rein of Ebony to the ground also, Gabe left the two animals and went to the creek to fetch the branches for Ezra's splint.

It was the spring hunt in the valley of the Arkansa river by the people of the Mouache Ute band led by Stone Buffalo. Gabriel Stonecroft and Ezra Blackwell, longtime friends and fellow explorers and discoverers, together with their wives and children, had spent the winter with the Ute and joined the hunt that always occurred when the buffalo first migrated north into the fertile valley of the Arkansa river. Gabe had chosen to hunt with his Mongol bow, finding it easier to use than trying to reload his Ferguson rifle while on the move, but Ezra opted for his reliable Lancaster rifle. They had been in many buffalo hunts before and knew they were not without risk and obvious danger, recalling that last time it was Gabe that was hurt.

When Gabe returned, the women had removed Ezra's buckskin tunic and exposed a few other scrapes and lumps, while the sweat made his black skin glisten in the sun. The worst of his wounds appeared to be the already bandaged gouge, although it was obvious, he had a couple broken ribs. He winced with every breath, but his eyes were open, and he was conscious. His head lay in Dove's lap while Cougar readied the wide strips of buckskin she would use to bind his ribs. Gabe looked at the broken leg, now exposed after Cougar had split his buckskins. He shook his head at the twisted and swollen form, then glanced at Cougar, as she said, "We will do this first. Then we will set his leg."

Gabe frowned, understanding that the pain would be difficult to handle, but with his ribs not bound, his reaction to the pain of setting his leg could do more damage. Gabe nodded, and dropped to one knee beside his friend, looked at him, "So, you thought you'd try one of my tricks and see what it was like to go flying, huh?"

Ezra started to laugh, winced at the pain, and said, "Don't do that . . . it hurts!" lifting his hand to his side.

With Dove and Cougar holding Ezra's upper torso by gripping his arms and shoulders, Gabe went to his feet and readied to set the leg. He examined it carefully, feeling the position of the bone ends, looked at the slight twist then seated himself at Ezra's feet. He put his foot at Ezra's crotch, grasped Ezra's foot in both hands, and nodded to Ezra. With eyes shut tight, an empty knife scabbard between his teeth, Ezra shook his head slightly, then nodded. With one hand at the heel, the other over the instep, Gabe slowly pulled, feeling the bone grate against bone, watching the movement beneath the skin. When the leg bone appeared in place, he twisted the foot and leg, aligning the break, then slowly released the pressure. He felt the muscles in the leg relax as Ezra lost consciousness, and satisfied with the set, Gabe nodded to Cougar to start positioning the splints and bandages.

Gabe stood, watching his woman minister to his friend, and when she finished, she stood and came to his side. Gabe put his arm around her waist, watching Dove place a blanket over her man then stand. With both hands on her hips, she looked at Gabe, "We," nodding to Cougar, "must tend to the buffalo. You must use the travois and take him to the cabin and get him into bed. Then you can return to help with the meat."

Gabe frowned, but it was the way of the people for the women to do the butchering of the animals. They would join the women of the village in the work, skinning, gutting, and quartering the animals. And that was just the beginning of their labors. Once they returned to the village, they would make pemmican, jerky, and more, as well as using most of the rest of the carcass for tools and such. Very little of the carcass would go unused.

Gabe whistled for Wolf, the big black wolf that had been at their side since he was a pup when they found

him in the cavern behind their cabin in the Wind
River mountains. When he trotted to Gabe, blood
showed at his jowls where he had been feasting on
the offal of the kills. Gabe glanced to the sky to see
several turkey buzzards circling the feast below, and
a quick glance showed the coyotes, badgers, crows,
ravens, and magpies had cast aside their caution and
joined in the feast of the gut piles. It was the way of
the wilderness that he had grown to love. He grinned
as he remembered the time so long ago when he and
Ezra had set out from Philadelphia, bounty hunters
hot on their trail, and came to the western wilderness
of what was then called French Louisiana.

He glanced at the towering peaks of the Sawatch
Range of the Rocky Mountains, smiled at the majesty,
and went to fetch the big grey packhorse to drag the
travois, with Ezra aboard, back to their cabin. They
had labored long and hard last fall to build the cabin
that lay in the narrow valley below the chalk cliffs at
the foothills of the Sawatch range. They chose the
site when they came with the Mouache Ute to their
winter encampment and were planning to camp with
the people, but the cabin site was too appealing and the
thought of a hard winter in a hide lodge versus a warm
cabin convinced them to build their third cabin in the
mountains. It was a cozy and tight cabin that lay in
the shadow of the tall bluff at the base of the foothills.
With black timber and aspen abundant around them,

their cabin was well sheltered from the winter winds, and with the storage cave they found in the face of the bluff, they had spent a comfortable winter.

The buffalo hunt was the tradition of the people and necessary to replenish their stores for the coming season and would also provide meat for their trek to their summer encampment far to the north. Gabe and company had joined to help the people, planning to add to the kill and provide for many of the lodges that had no man to provide for them. The skirmish last summer with the Spanish expedition of gold hunters had taken a toll on the warriors, leaving many women and children without a man in their lodge. It was the custom of the Ute as well as most plains tribes, that the village always cared for their own and no one would go without. Some of those women had joined the lodge of another, becoming the second wife of a warrior, and some had found another partner to replace their lost husband, but still others needed help and it was only right that everyone, including Gabe, Ezra, and their women, would join in those efforts.

After the four of them loaded Ezra on the travois, Gabe looked at the sun, now standing high in midday, glanced at the women and said, "It'll take most of the afternoon to get to the cabin and back, providin' I don't run into any difficulty, and you know what a good patient he is," nodding at Ezra with a grin.

"Listen to you! After all the times you played it

sick or injured, it's my turn to get a little attention!"
declared Ezra, groaning with the effort of talking.
He grimaced at the pain in his side, reached for the
blanket and pulled it up a little. "Come on an' get this
thing movin', my bed's callin' me!" With a chuckle,
Gabe swung aboard Ebony, motioned to Wolf to take
the lead, and nudged Ebony to a walk, drawing the
lead line of the grey taut to start on their way back
to the cabin.

2 / TRENDING

The cabin was larger than most with three rooms on the ground floor, one for each of the couples and the main room with the fireplace and furniture. The children slept in the loft overlooking the main room. Ezra was on their bed and Dove sat at his side. Cougar and Gabe stood behind her as she removed the poultice. The wound started bleeding again, and Dove looked back at Cougar Woman, "We must sew it together. It will not heal this way."

It was late the same day of the hunt and although they worked by candle light, the ragged edged wound pulsed with blood flow. Cougar nodded and turned away to get her parfleche and paraphernalia for tending the wound. As a young woman she had studied with the shaman of her people, but had chosen the way of a warrior, and became the war leader of her people. But after meeting Gabe, she left the village and became his wife. Now, Dove deferred to Cougar for the stitching of the wound.

Cougar sat on the edge of the bed beside Ezra, touching and examining the wound. She glanced at Gabe, nodded, and waited until Gabe had moved to the other side of Ezra to restrain the patient. Cougar cleaned the wound with cloth, dabbing at the blood, and with needle and silk thread garnered from the trade goods of the Hudson Bay traders they encountered in the Bitterroots, she started. Gabe leaned over Ezra's torso, holding Ezra's arms above his head with both hands on his wrists, and watched as Cougar slid the needle into flesh and muscle.

She was very adept and soon finished, much to the relief of Ezra who said, "If you took another stitch, I'd prob'ly bit my lip off! Dadgum it, I think gettin' mauled by a grizzly couldn't hurt worse'n that did!" he grumbled as he tried to sit up straight but was stayed by the pain in his side from the broken ribs. He shook his head and lay back, looked at Gabe, "Guess you're gonna hafta do it all by yourself, partner!"

"Do all of what?" asked Gabe, frowning.

"You know, all them step'n fetchits the women have up their sleeves."

Gabe chuckled, "I think most of that's been done already. That long winter kept us busy with things. If we'd cleaned our rifles and pistols one more time, we'd prob'ly wear a hole in the barrels or sump'thin."

It had been a busy and long winter with snowfalls that exceeded three and four feet. They had stored up grass cuttings and more for the horses and repaired all the tack and gear throughout the long days. But when snow melted and spring brought grass and more, they had worked on the corrals and sheds and the brush-works that kept the animals in the upper meadow.

Gabe stood beside the bed, his long lanky frame overshadowing the others. He was just over six feet tall, broad shouldered, deep chested and uncommonly strong, with a shock of blonde hair over his angular face. Usually clean-shaven, he was considered a hand-some man. He looked down at his long-time friend who was more of a brother, and grinned, "I reckon I can handle it, you usually just watched anyway!"

Ezra shook his head grinning, brought his arm from under the blanket to grasp the corner post to pull himself up. Gabe often described his friend as barrel chested and strong as an ox. He was a hand shorter than Gabe, but outweighed him by twenty pounds, all muscle. His shoulders, arms and chest rippled with deep muscles, and his friendly smile showed laughing eyes and white teeth contrasted by his dark skin. His thick curly hair and color had earned him the name Black Buffalo, and his strength and fighting ability held true to his name. His chis-eled features and bearing marked him as a confident good-looking man with a storm just under the surface. The men had been friends since their youthful days of wild imaginations wandering together in the woods near Philadelphia. When Gabe was forced into a duel with the ne'er do well son of a prominent and wealthy family who had insulted his sister, the outcome of the man's death and a bounty placed on his head forced Gabe to leave to protect his family and Ezra willingly joined him in his flight. Now, a little more than six years later, they were family men in the wilderness of Louisiana territory.

Ezra looked at Gabe, frowned, "What's the matter? You look like you've eaten green persimmons!"

Gabe laughed, "As if there were persimmons in this country!"

"You know what I mean, out with it!"

Gabe glanced at the women, looked at Ezra and leaned against the door jamb, "Hawk that Screams told me some of the men saw a band of Comanche watching from the trees as the women butchered the buffalo."

"Comanche? I thought this was Ute country," countered Ezra, twisting to get comfortable as he sat up.

"It is, but we both know there is nothing preventing any other tribe from hunting where they want to, or raiding."

"Did anything happen, you know, any fighting?" asked Ezra, frowning.

"No, Hawk said they just sat their ponies and

watched, then disappeared into the trees. He said it was on the south end of the field. The river is back in those foothills, cuts through a canyon back there according to Hawk."

"I thought that was Arapaho country," replied Ezra.

"It is. But further south and east are the Kiowa and Comanche. If they had a hard winter, they might have to range further to hunt."

Cougar added, "There are also Jicarilla Apache to the south."

"Any of 'em friendly?" asked Gabe.

"Sometimes," answered Cougar, with a shrug, letting a slight smile tug at the corner of her mouth.

"Well, we better hope they're all friendly, at least until I get outta this bed!" declared Ezra. "Now, how 'bout you all gettin' outta here so this poor wounded and broken patient can get some rest!"

Gabe and Cougar started for the door, followed by Dove, until Ezra said, "Not you, woman!" reaching out as if to grab her, "I need you here," patting the bed beside him, smiling.

Dove laughed, glanced at Cougar, "It's nice to be needed." She turned back to the bed, then called over her shoulder, "Could you check on the little ones?"

Cougar answered, "You know I will."

It was just past midnight when the cold nose of Wolf brought Gabe instantly awake. The big wolf padded through the open door of their room and went to the front door of the cabin, scratched at the door as Gabe grabbed his rifle standing beside it and followed Wolf into the night. With a long leap, Wolf hit the ground running around the house toward the upper meadow. They took the trail through the trees, Gabe's long legs keeping pace with Wolf, and halted at the tree line, the half-moon showing bright on the grassy meadow. The horses were skittish and standing with their butts to the brushworks nearest Gabe, Ebony with ears up and forward, staring at the far trees as he danced nervously beside the appaloosa mare.

Gabe glanced at the horses, then searched the flats and the trees for any movement and was startled by the raspy caterwauling wail of a mountain lion, followed by the choked huffing, and growling that was muted by the trees. But something about the cry was not quite right to the seasoned ears of the mountain man Gabe. He glanced to Wolf who was in his attack stance, head lower than his shoulders, orange eyes piercing the darkness, jowl dripping with saliva. Wolf turned to Gabe and back to the distance beyond the meadow.

Gabe listened, waiting for another scream of the cougar, but none came. He shook his head, *Either that's an old and maybe injured cat, or . . .* but he wasn't certain what else it could be that would make that sound. *If it were horse thieves, they wouldn't want to startle the horses before they could take them, or would they?* He glanced down to Wolf, reached down to stroke his scruff, and spoke softly, "I think we got some prowling Comanche!"

"They want to stampede the horses," came a quiet voice from behind him. Gabe recognized the soft voice of Cougar Woman, shook his head as he turned, "Why am I not surprised that you're here?"

"It is usually you and Ezra that come out, but he's still sleeping," she grinned as she stepped closer.

Gabe drew her close in a quick embrace, then spoke in a whisper, "I reckon they'll open up the brush yonder," nodding toward the upper end of the pasture, "and the one that made that scream will come down here to spook 'em thataway."

"There will be more there," answered Cougar, pointing with her chin to the far end, "you and Wolf take them, I will kill a puma!"

3 / CATAMOUNT

Wolf padded through the trees, eyes accustomed to the darkness. Gabe followed close behind moving just as quietly, using the deep shadows and the black timber to his advantage, the lances of moonlight dancing in the dark before him. As they neared the upper end of the pasture, both stopped, listening. The movement of brush whispered, hissed words passed between the three or four figures. Wolf dropped to his belly, a low growl rumbling, glancing back to Gabe, as the man dropped to one knee beside him. Gabe dropped a hand to Wolf's scruff, watching the shadowy forms as they pulled aside the branches and brush that had been woven as a barrier to keep the horses from wandering into the woods, prompting them to be secured in the grassy meadow. It was obvious they planned to steal all the horses, antici-pating the stampede when they came from the lower pasture to flee from the screams of the catamount.

Cougar spoke softly to the horses, calming them with her presence and words, then stepped back into the trees. The horses still showed a little nervousness, heads up, ears forward, glancing around and huddling close together. Cougar expected the warrior that had mimicked the cry of the mountain lion to stealthily make his way around the pasture, using the trees and darkness to conceal his approach, and thought he might even have the hide of a cougar for the scent and even the appearance. She stood in the shadow of the tall ponderosa, watching the forest freckled with the shafts of moonlight, and listened. The whisper of buckskin rubbing past a low branch, the muffled crunch of dried pine needles, would not have been heard by a less-seasoned warrior, but the crafty Cougar Woman knew what she heard, and waited, an arrow nocked in the bow string as she held it across her chest.

Gabe touched the butt of the Bailes over/under pistol in his belt. Moved his hand back to the fore stock of the Ferguson rifle, and with it held close to his buckskins, he waited for another movement of the brush and brought it to full cock. As he watched the figures, he was certain there were four, and he mentally calculated his moves, judging which of the men was the most confident and probably the most dangerous. Gabe quickly scanned the slight clearing, saw one man motioning to the others, and moved closer behind him.

Suddenly the piercing scream came from the lower end of the pasture, prompting the men to quicken their movement, pulling the brush clear. Gabe lifted his rifle and barked, "Don't move!"

But the men dove for their weapons, and Gabe's rifle bucked as it roared, racketing the sound of death through the trees, and bouncing off the mountainside. Grey smoke belched into the shaft of moonlight, as the bullet crashed into the skull of the leader of the raiders, exploding out the other side and splattering blood and detritus into the trees. Before the smoke cleared, Gabe stood the rifle against the tree and brought his pistol up, cocking it in the same move and brought it to bear on the next warrior, just as an arrow buried itself in the trunk of the tree beside him. The pistol blasted before the echo of the rifle shot stilled, filling the darkness with its roar and the grass with blood as the bullet smashed the bone hair pipe breast plate and shattered the solar plexus of the warrior.

Gabe lowered the pistol, keeping his wary eyes on the other two warriors as he rotated the barrels of the pistol, brought the hammer to a cock and lifted the weapon, bringing the shiny brass blade to bear on the third warrior, just as the man came to his feet, bringing his lance back for a throw, but the .54 caliber ball shattered the bone in his shoulder, driving him back and dropping his lance. The fourth man had disappeared into the trees, but Gabe snatched up the Ferguson, spun the trigger guard to open the breech, and rapidly reloaded, closed the breech and snapped open the pan and primed the rifle, snapped the frizzen down and eared back the hammer.

The scream like the cry of a cougar was choked off when an arrow drove into the neck of the man, silencing him as he dropped the hide and grabbed at the arrow. Blood spurted around the shaft and covered his hands as he dropped to his knees, frightened eyes flaring wide, as he searched for his assailant. Cougar Woman stepped from the darkness, another arrow nocked, and moved close to the man who was gasping for air. She spoke in the language of her people, a sardonic grin painting her face, "My name is Cougar Woman. You tried to be a Cougar and a Cougar killed you!"

Wolf had started for the second warrior, but Gabe's bullet struck first. The big black wolf started for another that had taken off at a run into the trees. Gabe had moved through the trees as he reloaded, but never took his eyes from the clearing nor the wounded warrior. He paused, listening, watching, and waited. The only sound was the movement of the horses, who had shied away from the opening when the gunfire blasted, and with a glance toward the opening, Gabe slowly moved that way, wanting to keep any horse that might be more afraid of a panther than the gunfire from trying his luck at escaping. He dropped to one knee beside the tree nearest the opening, watching, and listening. When he heard the movement of a horse deeper in the trees and away from the meadow, he believed it to be the one man that had disappeared into the darkness, and Gabe pierced the night with his sharp whistle to summon Wolf back, then quickly moved to a different position. Gabe waited, listening as the horse moved away, then quickened its pace as the sound faded.

The moaning of the wounded man came from the edge of the trees, but Gabe did not know how badly the man had been hit, knowing that even a wounded man is a dangerous one. Gabe picked his way carefully through the edge of the trees, moving a few steps, stopping, and listening. Ragged breathing intermingled with muted moans told Gabe the man was near, and he watched carefully until he could make out the prone figure, lying on his side, struggling for breath, and fighting to stifle his moans. The low growl told Gabe Wolf had already found the wounded man and was waiting for his signal to attack. Gabe stepped from the trees behind the figure and spoke softly, "Do not move," knowing the man probably did not understand English, but would possibly comprehend the meaning by Gabe's actions. He also knew his words would stay Wolf from an attack.

He stepped around the wounded warrior, keeping the muzzle of the rifle aimed at his midriff, then saw the man's frightened eyes lift to him, and the man instinctively pulled back when Wolf showed himself beside Gabe. Instead of the expected anger and contempt, Gabe saw fear and helplessness. The wounded man held his hand at his shoulder, blood trickling through his fingers and pooling on the ground before him. The man was obviously weak from loss of blood, but if his wound were tended, he could survive. Gabe lifted the man's knife from the scabbard at his belt, looked for other weapons, saw the bow lying nearby, the quiver still at the man's back.

Gabe stood his rifle against the tree, and knelt before the man, his knife at the ready, making the warrior's eyes flutter in fear, probably thinking Gabe was about to slit his throat. But Gabe reached out to gently pull the man's hand away from the wound, glanced around for a place with more moonlight, and stood, just as Cougar Woman came into the open. He looked at her, "This'uns hurt pretty bad, but if he's tended, will live. One got away, two others are dead," he pointed with his chin to the crumpled forms lying in the shadows where they fell.

"The one that made the cry of the catamount, will make the cry no more," replied Cougar Woman, looking at the wounded man. She glanced at the others, then to Gabe, "Cut wide strips of buckskin from their leggings. We will bind his wounds and take him to the cabin."

Gabe nodded, went to one of the downed warriors and cut the leggings into long wide strips, returned to Cougar as she knelt beside the man, holding a quickly fashioned poultice made from the nearby arrowleaf, using the sap directly on the wound and the leaves for the poultice. When Gabe returned with the buckskin strips, she instructed him to catch one of the horses to transport the warrior and wrapped the man's shoulder tightly.

Gabe decided to find the horses of the warriors and soon returned, leading four. He put three in the meadow, pulled the brush back across the opening, and helped Cougar lift the wounded man to the back of the fourth horse. With Cougar leading the animal and Gabe walking alongside to keep the wounded man aboard, they soon returned to the cabin.

With the now unconscious warrior on a blanket on the porch, and Cougar aided by candlelight held by Gabe, she cleaned the wound and replaced the temporary bandage with a poultice made from goldenrod and bear root. Once the bandage was secured and the arm and shoulder bound tightly, Gabe tied the man's free arm to the porch post with rawhide. Cougar covered the patient with another blanket, and with Wolf by their side, they entered the cabin, shutting and securing the door behind them.

4 / WOUNDED

"In the days of my father's fathers, those that are known as Comanche, were part of the Shoshone people. When our people lived in the land of many waters and north, those people left and went to the south. Their words and ours were the same. Perhaps he," pointing with her chin, Cougar Woman continued, "will know our words."

After the restless night and little sleep after the fight with the raiders, they had risen early. Gabe checked on the wounded man who was bound on the porch, returned inside for his morning brew of roasted chicory and what little coffee that remained. He sat at the table as Cougar spoke, "I do not know if his shoulder will heal. The bone was broken," she touched her shoulder to point out the location of the wound, "and he might not use it."

"He hasn't said much, just looked at me like he

wanted to cut my throat," responded Gabe, sipping his coffee. "How's your other patient? His shoulder gonna mend alright?"

"Yes, it will be hard to keep him down, even with his broken leg." She sat down opposite her man, "What will we do with that one?" nodding toward the porch and the captive Comanche.

Gabe shook his head, "Dunno. Maybe keep him here till he heals up, then send him on his way." He looked up at Cougar, "Reckon we might learn a little 'bout his people while he's here?"

"If he talks," answered Cougar. "The others should be buried," she suggested, referring to the dead Comanche raiders. "Their people might come looking for them, and we have their horses with ours."

"Hmmm, yeah. I might need you to come with me, but I don't like leavin' that one here with the kids and Dove. Ezra's not much help."

"I heard that!" shouted Ezra's voice through the open door to their room. "Get me a crutch an' I'll get outta here!" But his protests were followed by a grunt and a wince, obviously from his rambunctious arousal that reminded him of his broken ribs.

Gabe retorted, "You just stay there and guard that bed! Don't want nobody stealin' it out from under you!"

Ezra's grumbling was easily heard as Dove came from the room and went to the youngsters playing on the buffalo robe and blankets on the floor in the corner of the main room. She shook her head and grinned, laughing at the antics of her man, but pleased that he was feeling more like himself.

Gabe motioned for Cougar to join him as he started from the cabin. They stepped onto the porch, looked to the mouth of the canyon to see the sun just showing its many colors of early morning and then looked to the wounded man. He had sat up beside the porch post and was also watching the sun rise, but he turned to face Gabe and Cougar with a scowl. As they were seated, Cougar spoke in the tongue of the Shoshone, "Were you greeting the new day and the Creator?"

The man frowned, surprise showing on his face to hear the woman speak his tongue. He growled, "You are not *Numunuu!* But you speak our tongue."

Cougar let the makings of a grin lift the corner of her mouth, "I am Shoshone! Your people were our people in the times of our grandfathers."

The man frowned and Gabe noticed he was a young man. Although fully grown, showing little of the youthful look or manner, it was evident by his features, face, and more that he was a young man. In the darkness of the fight, little could be distinguished of the raiders, but in the full light of day Gabe guessed him to be sixteen or seventeen summers.

Cougar added, "I am Cougar Woman, war leader

of the Tukkutikka Shoshone. This is my man, Spirit Bear. Our friends inside are Black Buffalo and his woman, Grey Dove of the Kuccuntikka Shoshone." She paused, then added, "What are you called and who are your people?"

"I am White Knife of the *Yaparuhka* Comanche."

"Your people have come far north for your raids, why?"

"It was a bad season of cold and snow and dry. We followed the buffalo." He looked from Cougar to Gabe and to Wolf who lay between them, watching the man. "I have not known any man that keeps a wolf," he stated, looking up at Gabe.

Gabe grinned, "We don't keep him, he keeps us. He has been with us since he was a pup and is a good friend."

White Knife frowned, dropped his eyes, and quietly asked, "Those that were with me?"

Gabe answered, "The one like the cougar, was killed," with a slight nod to Cougar Woman, "Your leader and one other also were killed. One man, smaller than the others, took his horse and left," explained Gabe, motioning with his hand of the man's leaving.

White Knife frowned, "Where are the others?" looking around.

"Others?"

"There were many that came against us in the dark."

Gabe slowly shook his head, "No, that was just me

and Wolf here. He chased after the one that made it to his horse, but I called him back."

White Knife looked from Gabe to Cougar and back, frowned and looked somewhat sideways at Gabe, trying to discern if what he said was truthful. He asked, "You came alone against four?"

Gabe nodded, leaning forward in his chair to look directly at the man. "Ummhumm, now, how far away was the rest of your war party?"

"It was not a war party. We were on a hunt, but when we saw the village hunters and their kill," nodding to the lodges of the Ute that lay in the valley bottom below and upstream of the cabin, "we watched from the trees."

"We saw you. Your people should have come down and shared the meat. The headman of the village is Stone Buffalo. He is a man of peace."

"The Ute and the Comanche are enemies!" he spat.

Gabe leaned back and sipped his coffee, glanced to Cougar with a slight nod, prompting her to go inside and fetch White Knife some coffee. He looked hard at White Knife, "While you are in our lodge, the Ute are our friends!" Gabe believed White Knife was doing nothing more than regurgitating the attitude of his fellow warriors and had probably never met a Ute warrior. *That seems to be the way it is, so easy to hate someone, call them your enemy, and never really know them,* thought Gabe as he sipped his hot brew, looking at White Knife over the rim of the cup.

"Your shoulder is alright?" asked Gabe, nodding to the wound.

"It will heal."

"Cougar Woman treated your wound and tried to fit the bones together. She said there are many pieces there and it might not heal right," explained Gabe, still holding the cup before his face, his elbows on the arms of the chair.

White Knife frowned, looked down at the bandages and bindings, winced as he tried to move it. He looked at Gabe, a touch of fear showing in his eyes, "It must heal," he declared, as if saying so would make it so.

When Cougar returned with a cup for White Knife, she bent to untie the rawhide to free his arm, but before loosing it, she looked at him, "If you try anything," and turned to nod at Wolf, "He will tear you apart and finish by ripping out your throat."

White Knife's eyes flared as he glanced past Cougar to see Wolf sit up and curl his lip as if anticipating his attack. White Knife said, "I will do nothing."

Cougar untied the binding, handed him the cup and sat back beside Gabe. They watched as he sipped at the coffee, grinned and nodded to Cougar, "We have traded with the Comancheros for this coffee. It is good."

Gabe lowered his cup and began, "We need to tend

to the bodies of your friends today. Do you think you could ride along?"

White Knife frowned, "You would do this?"

"Of course. We have respect for the dead. They should be buried proper."

"I will ride with you."

5 / BURIAL

Three bodies, each wrapped in the blankets that had been a part of the gear on the remaining horses, draped over the backs of the three Indian ponies. Mustangs that had been caught and trained by the very men that now made their last ride into the mountains, trailed behind Gabe, Cougar, and White Knife. Wolf led the way as they took the trail at the edge of the bluff, pointing up canyon. "There's a cut at the end of that ridge," nodding to the long finger ridge that jutted out from the base of the higher mountain range, "I don't know if there's any caves, but it's mighty rocky and there's overhangs that can be kicked down, deep gulches that might serve."

"It is the custom of my people to bury the dead as you said, it does not have to be a cave, but a cave is easier," explained White Knife. The Comanche warrior was determined to make this trek to honor his fallen comrades, but it was evident he was growing weak and would not be able to travel much further and still make the ride back to the cabin.

"It right up there," stated Gabe as he pointed to the narrow draw emerging from the flanks of the timbered mountains. A thin stand of aspen waved like a banner of invitation, marking the narrow defile. A narrow game trail hung from the steeper slope and offered a path into the cut. Wolf paused, looked over his shoulder at the others, and at the slight nod from Gabe, he started up the trail. Less than half a mile up the draw, a steep talus stood like a grey ogre, forcing the small stream to wend around the point. Gabe reined up, frowning, stepped down and walked to the thick brush at the base of the rocks. After tussling with a stubborn chokecherry bush, he stood, turned around, "Looks like we found what we need. But we'll hafta be careful puttin' 'em in there, this rock's a mite unstable."

Although White Knife tried to help, his bound-up shoulder limited what he could handle, and finally yielded to Gabe and Cougar Woman as they wrestled the three bundles into the shallow cavity. With barely enough room to lie the three beside one another, Gabe motioned Cougar away from the mouth of the depression. He climbed the side of the slope and carefully worked his way above the cave, sat down and with his feet began pushing rocks and debris down to cover the opening. The small rockslide crashed down, causing a cloud of dust to rise, but Gabe was able to slide down easily.

They stood a moment until Gabe asked, "Does your custom call for any words or . . .?"

White Knife glanced at Gabe, shook his head and added, "The mourning of their families will begin when they know of their fate."

On their return, Gabe told White Knife, "If you can travel tomorrow, you can take these horses back to their people."

White Knife frowned, "But I am your captive!"

"No, we just tied you last night so we could sleep peacefully. Your wounds have been tended, Cougar will probably want to change the bandage, but you may return to your people."

"Why would you do this? If you were a captive of my people, you would be tortured or made a slave or . . ." he shrugged.

"We are not your enemy. You and your fellow warriors were on a raid to steal horses, but it cost the lives of your friends and you are wounded. There has been enough."

Cougar added, "But if you or your people come against us again, there will be much bloodshed, and more will be put in the ground."

"I will tell my father of this."

"Your father?" asked Gabe, frowning.

"Yes. My father is Old Owl, the leader of our village. My brother, Black Bear, is the war leader and the leader of the hunting party. The warrior that led this raid," nodding toward the upper pasture with the horses, "is in the ground. There were four young warriors and the one that led. He had promised an easy raid and honors and horses for the young men. He was foolish."

"It would be best if you wait until tomorrow, you should rest," suggested Cougar.

"I must return. Rattling Voice is the one that left. He will tell the people that I am dead, and I would not have my mother and father mourn."

With the three horses on a long lead, White Knife accepted Gabe's help in getting back on his horse. Cougar handed him a pouch with smoked meat and biscuits, and with a nod, White Knife rode from the clearing and the cabin. Gabe looked at Cougar as they turned back to the house, "You think he'll make it?"

"Yes, but what his people will do, I do not know."

"There has been much talk in the village about you," began Stone Buffalo. He sat at the fire opposite Gabe, the old headman Walks on Mountains beside him. "They say you rode with a Comanche and took three bodies into the canyon and returned with only the Comanche." He paused as he looked at Gabe. The women were busy preparing the evening meal as they worked in the cabin and Ezra was still abed. The fire in the clearing was more of a gathering place, but in the warmer times the women often used the outside fire for cooking. The men had brought a couple smooth grey cottonwood logs from below to use as benches at the fire.

Gabe looked up at Stone Buffalo, "What your people say is true." He paused, then glanced from Walks on Mountains to Stone Buffalo, "There was a band of raiders that came late in the night two nights ago, they were after our horses. We killed some, one was wounded, the one that rode with us to bury the dead, and one ran away."

"Did they take any horses?" asked Walks.

"No, we put a stop to that right away."

Stone Buffalo frowned, "Black Buffalo is injured, and he could not fight."

Gabe grinned, "Cougar Woman was with me."

Stone Buffalo slowly lifted his head in a nod, then asked, "The wounded one that rode with you?"

"We sent him back to his people with the horses of the other warriors."

Both Stone Buffalo and Walks on Mountains, frowned as Stone Buffalo asked, "Sent him back to his people?"

Gabe just nodded while he used a stick to stir the coals of the fire.

With a glance to Walks on Mountains, Stone Buffalo looked at Gabe, "We came to tell you we, our village, are leaving to return to our summer camp. Our hunt was good, and we have much meat. There is to be a gathering of our people and our village is anxious for the high country to visit our friends and family."

"We thought that would happen soon," answered Gabe. "But with Ezra down and needin' time to heal, we'll be staying here." He lifted his eyes to the white cliffs across the valley, the rising moon painting them with a hint of blue, "We like it here, so, if you come back next fall, we might just be here waiting."

Walks on Mountains asked, "Will the Comanche return?"

"I don't know, the one we sent away, White Knife, was surprised, but I think he'll speak to his people. His father is Old Owl, the leader of their village and hopefully they'll choose to leave us alone. But we did kill a few of their young warriors . . ."

"The Comanche are a fierce people, their warriors are good fighters," added Stone Buffalo. "You would do well to be watchful, perhaps even leave this valley for a time."

Gabe shrugged, again stirring the coals, but he knew Ezra would be at least another week before he could ride, and perhaps not then. Even if he could, where would they go, and why? Gabe stood as Stone

Buffalo and Walks on Mountains rose to leave. The old man turned back, "You," with a nod toward the cabin to include the others, "will always be welcome in our village."

"And you and your people will always be welcome at my fire," answered Gabe as he watched the two leaders of the Mouache Ute people leave the clearing. He sat for a moment longer, thinking of the time spent with the people of the Mouache, the battle they shared, the time and hunts together, the friendships made. It seemed like they were always leaving new friends behind on their endless quest to explore and discover. Their lives had been enriched by all the friends they made throughout the wild country, but they were all too often friends they would never see again. His reverie was interrupted by Cougar's voice as she called from the cabin that the meal was ready. He stood, smiling, as he saw his beautiful wife standing beside the porch post, arms folded, and smiling as she watched her man in the dim light of the moon, walk to her, arms outstretched for her embrace.

6 / YAPARUHKA

It was a confused White Knife that rode from the cabin of the white man and his people. All he had been
taught about those that were not of the *Yaparuhka* or
the Comanche, were enemies of the people. He had
known his people to fight the Apache, Kiowa, Pawnee,
Arapaho, and Ute. He had heard the old people talk of
those that wore iron shirts and hats and came from the
south, the first ones that had the horse and weapons
of thunder, and even they were the enemy. But now
this white man and his woman has shown himself to
be a friend and respectful of the ways of the people,
even after he and his warriors had mounted a raid to
steal their horses. *And what will my father think when
I tell him these things?* He winced, both at the thought
of his father's reaction and the pain in his shoulder.

He had been riding since about mid-day, and if he
did not meet the rest of the hunting party, he would

need to go all the way to the summer encampment of his people, a location that was further north than they had ever summered but promised to be a fruitful time for the people. White Knife began to look for a likely place to camp for the night, he was tired, his wound had started bleeding again, and the horses needed rest. He was at the mouth of the canyon that swallowed the Arkansa river, the beginnings of the long mountain range known as the Sangre de Cristo shouldered high above the south edge of the wide fertile valley. White Knife would hold to the north shore of the river and chose the mouth of a gulch that still carried a thin trickle of water from the country of the crater, known as *Po-a-cat-le-pi-le-carre,* one of many mountains or craters known as Medicine Rock.

He made a simple camp in the lee of a thick cluster of juniper, a fire just big enough to heat the water he would use to wash his wound and to give him some coffee, the handful of grounds hoarded from the last trade his people had with the Comancheros. He peeled off the bandage, and washed away the remains of the poultice, cleaning the wound and wiping away the dried blood and the fresh that still bled. Cougar Woman, the white man's Shoshone woman, had given him a fresh poultice and bandage to use and he easily applied it and struggled one-handed to bind it all tight. Once done, he sat back, relieved, and began munching on the smoked meat she had put in his pack. He wondered about them, if he would ever see them again, and his mind returned to his father, Old Owl, and what he might say about those people.

He kept to the trail that shadowed the river through the bit of a canyon, sometimes being no more than a shelf high above the rushing water, but easily traveled by the horses. With four animals strung out behind him, he took his time and enjoyed the country. More than once he kicked up some mule deer that had gone to the river for their daily trek for water and green graze. With little more than bunch grass and sage in the rocky hills, the greenery near the river was worth the daily trek for deer, bighorn sheep, and a few elk and antelope. Coyotes, rabbits, and other smaller animals were plentiful, as were rattlesnakes that liked sunning on the hot rocks beside the trail.

The sun was just shy of its high point in the day when White Knife broke from the mouth of the canyon and the wide green slopes that fell from the high mountains and lay like a blanket on the south side of the river stretching to the foothills that skirted the Sangre de Cristo mountains. This was the upper end of Comancheria, the land of the people. He stopped, shielded his eyes from the mid-day sun and looked to the village that was nestled below the shoulders of the long flat mesas that came from the mountains, and close to the river. The bluffs offered protection from the cold winds that came from the snow-capped peaks, and the nearby river afforded water and ample graze for the horse herd.

White Knife grinned and goaded his mount forward, pointing them to the wide shallow crossing that held a long island and lay about a half-mile upstream of the village. The crossing was easy and when he climbed the slight bank away from the thick cottonwoods, he turned toward the village. Within moments, he was spotted, and two riders came toward him. As they neared, he lifted his hand high, and the riders came alongside. "Aiiieee, it is White Knife! He has returned from the dead!" declared the one known as Crazy Hawk.

The second rider, Black Bear, recognized White Knife and came closer, "My brother returns. Our father and mother will be happy to see you! Our mother was beginning her mourning for her youngest son!" He paused, looking at the horses on the long lead, "These are the horses of the others?"

"Yes. They have crossed over and their bodies were buried."

"I see you have a bandage, is it bad?" asked Black Bear as he rode alongside his brother.

"It will heal, but maybe not the same. It was a bullet from a rifle."

"Our council had been talking of a war party to seek vengeance against the Ute."

"It was not the Ute. Did Rattling Voice say this?"

"Yes! He said you and the others were ambushed by a great band of Ute and he killed three before he fled. He said all of you were killed before he left."

White Knife shook his head, sucked in a deep breath, and glared at his brother. "Have you ever known Rattling Voice to be truthful? Or to be a great warrior?"

Black Bear glanced sideways at his brother, letting a slow grin split his face, "I did not want to believe him, but the others had no one else to speak for them."

"I must see our father before this war party leaves!" declared White Knife. "It will be hard for him to hear what I have to say."

"What is that?" asked Black Bear.

"Come to the council and hear for yourself."

Although it was not the custom for just any one to address the council of elders and headmans of the people, but a warrior returning from the dead deserved to be heard. Before White Knife spoke, he looked around the circle at the venerable leaders of the people. These were men that had repeatedly proven themselves in battle and shown their wisdom as they led the people. Most had at least some grey in their hair, some with hair that touched the ground as they sat about the circle. All with battle scars, some with skin wrinkled with age, others with skin taut over thick muscles, tattoos covered chests, arms and even faces. When Old Owl lifted his arms, quiet fell like a blanket, and the leader spoke, "My son, White Knife, has returned after we were told he had been killed in a great battle. He has much to tell us." The headman slowly lowered his arms as he looked around at the others, the stern expression demanding their attention and respect.

White Knife stood, "The warrior you know as a great taker of horses," he began, choosing not to use the names of the dead out of respect for their memory and to not summon the spirit of evil from the graves, "said we should raid the village of the Ute and take their horses." He held out one hand, all fingers extended, "Four young warriors anxious to gain horses to trade and take a wife, agreed to go with the leader. His plan was for the young warrior who was known for his way of making the cry of the mountain lion, to make that cry, then circle around to the lower end of the meadow that held the horses, but he had led us, not to the herd of the Ute, but to a smaller herd that had a great black stallion that he wanted. There were some great horses there and we thought we could easily take them. When he made the cry, the horses spooked, as planned. When they went to the lower end, we began tearing down the brush and more that held the horses. The scream of the mountain lion was heard, a voice came from the dark. We grabbed our weapons, but the man shot the rifle, and pistol, and in that much time," snapping his fingers, "two were dead, I was wounded, and one had run away like a rabbit!" he spat.

White Knife looked around the circle of men who sat stunned at the report until Old Owl asked, "Did the one that made the cry of the mountain lion die?"

White Knife dropped his eyes to the ground, then looked up at his father, "One man, a white man, killed the two with me and wounded me. His woman was in the woods waiting for the one that made the sound of the cougar and killed him."

"But how did you escape?" asked Black Bear.

"The white man and his woman took me to their lodge. She tended my wounds and bound my shoulder. At first light, we gathered the bodies of the dead, wrapped them in blankets and buried them in the mountains. When we came back to the man's lodge, his woman tended my wound, gave me food and more for my wound, and the white man put me on my horse, gave me the horses of the others, and said he was not our enemy. His name is Spirit Bear, his woman is a war leader of the Shoshone, her name is Cougar Woman. His friend is Black Buffalo, and his woman is Grey Dove of the Shoshone."

The council members frowned, looked from one to another and to the headman, Old Owl, who also showed a little consternation as he considered what his son had said happened. As they spoke to one another in low tones, even whispers, one man toward the rear of the lodge was obviously upset and spoke up, "I believe White Knife is confused. Perhaps his wound had affected his thinking. But what is true is my brother was killed by this white man, Spirit Bear, and I believe the Ute people were part of the battle. One man could not have turned away five of our warriors, even with his woman helping him. We must mount a war party and go after this man and his Ute friends, our dead brothers' blood cries out for vengeance!" he snarled. The speaker was the man known as Many Bears, a proven warrior, but never one that rose as a leader, and was more often known as one that provoked others into fights and trouble.

"This man gave me my life, and my freedom, and the horses of our warriors. He and his friends are not the enemies of the *Numunuu*. We are the *Pibianigwai* people of the *Yaparuhka* band of the people. We do not make war against those that have proven themselves to be friends of the people. When they killed our warriors, they were defending their horses and their home against those of us who would take them. They are no different than us," he pointed at himself and the others in the circle, "who would keep our own families and property from those that would steal from us." He breathed heavily, looking exasperated and showing his weakness from his wound, and added. "For us to go against these would not only be wrong, he and his are great warriors and we could lose many of our warriors just so Many Bears could have his vengeance when none is required."

White Knife staggered as he sat down, steadied by his brother, Black Bear, and once seated, he looked around the circle, seeing many heads nodding and agreement shown. Old Owl lifted his arms and said, "We will consider the words of White Knife and the cry of Many Bears. Let us meet again after first light of the day following." Several nodded, and all rose to leave the lodge of Old Owl. As they filed out, the mumbled words of Many Bears could be heard, as he growled and spoke against what White Knife had spoken, but nothing could be done against the man, for he was entitled to his thoughts.

7 / HORSES

The cabin sat on the shoulder above the thicket of aspen that bordered the creek in the bottom of the valley. Behind the cabin and butted up to the bluff stood the tack shed, lean-to, and storage shed that opened to the dug-out in the face of the bluff that held their cold storage. A corral stretched along the face of the bluff with one side open to the tack shed and lean-to for shelter for the horses. Past the corral and with a fenced alley leading up the slope of the bluff, was the beginning of the upper meadow. Gabe led the appaloosa and steeldust from the meadow to the corral to begin the day's work with the horses. The appaloosa, a colt out of the Appy mare and Ebony, had been gelded last fall by Gabe and Ezra and had been tamed under the experienced and gentle touch of Cougar Woman. The steeldust gelding had been broke to ride but used as a pack animal, however now they had other plans for the little mustang.

As Gabe led the horses into the corral, he was greeted by Cougar Woman who stood ready with a small saddle she had been working on through the winter months. It had a rawhide covered wooden frame with rabbit fur padding underneath. Smooth leather covered the seat and pommel and cantle, the saddle horn was the height of two hands and hung with fringe and just the right height and size for the boy. Gabe tethered the appaloosa to the fence rail, led the steeldust to the tack shed and began saddling him. He glanced to the fence to see his son, Bobcat, sitting beside Ezra's son, Chipmunk, both watching and showing their excitement. While Cougar was busy with the Appy, Gabe led the steeldust to the fence and lifted a grinning Chipmunk into his daddy's saddle. This was not the first time for the boy, but as is the way with youngsters, every time in the saddle is just as exciting as the first time, perhaps more so as the previous experience is enjoyed again.

"Now, here's the rein, but I'll hold on by the bit. You know what to do, so let's just walk around the corral," instructed Gabe. He glanced to Ezra, who leaned against the fence, the crutch fashioned from the aspen sapling under his arm keeping the weight off the broken and healing leg.

The proud papa grinned and offered his own encouragement, "You're lookin' good son!" Ezra leaned down to look under the top rail, his elbow on the second rail for support, his broad smile showing through the rails. He glanced to Dove who stood by his side, "A born horseman, that's what he is, a born horseman."

As he spoke he saw Gabe release his hold on the bridle, and continue walking beside the horse's head, glancing back at Chipmunk and nodding. The boy grinned at Gabe, "Can I trot him?"

"As long as you stay by the fence and don't get too close to Bobcat!" answered Gabe as he stepped away from the horse. He watched as the short legs of Chipmunk bounced, kicking at the sides of the gelding. The steeldust picked up his pace and started at a trot, hugging the rail fence, but conscious of the boy atop. With one hand on the loop rein, the other on his thigh, the boy clenched the edge of the pommel with his knees and rocked with the rhythm of the gait. He smiled broadly, no fright showing in his eyes, no thought of losing his seat and falling to the ground, just the joy of a boy and his horse.

After Chipmunk made several circuits of the corral, Gabe motioned him to stop and the boy pulled the horse to a slow stop. The boy arched his back, sitting straight and tall, and looked at his Mom and Dad with a broad smile, the expression soliciting their praise. Ezra chuckled, "You did great Chipmunk! Proud of you boy! Bring him on over here, son," motioning to the boy to come close.

Dove bounced on her toes, and quietly clapped her excitement and pride, but as the boy neared, she sobered and spoke softly to Ezra, "He should let Bobcat ride now," nodding toward the waiting Cougar as she stood with the Appy in the lean-to, waiting.

Dove stepped up on the fence, reached over the top and helped Chipmunk to stretch from the saddle to the top rail while Gabe took the bridle in hand to lead the steeldust away. As Gabe tethered the little gelding in the lean-to, Cougar led the Appy to the fence and reached up to help Bobcat off the top rail. She stood the boy on the ground beside the horse, then bent down on one knee beside the boy. "Now, I will hold him while you climb up."

Bobcat smiled at his mom, reached up tip toed to grab the end of the tie down near the cantle of the saddle, and with the other hand grabbing at the girth, he stepped up on his mother's knee, grabbed the tie down beside the pommel. He stretched up and put his left foot in the small stirrup and stepped up, swinging his leg over the cantle, and sat in the seat, grinning and proud as he looked at his mom. He accepted the rein from Cougar, and as she gripped the end of the rein and the bridle, she started walking the Appy around the corral.

"Look Daddy!" declared the boy, waving to his father who stood beside the fence watching every move.

"You're doin' fine, son, fine!" It was not the first

ride for Bobcat, but it was the first in the new saddle that fit him and gave him added confidence. His first rides had been bareback on Ebony with Dad holding tight to the boy, but he had soon gained the confidence to handle the big black without Dad's hand on him. But this Appy would be his very own horse and even though he had ridden the Appy bareback with Dad beside him, this was even better.

Cougar smiled up at her son, "You have the rein, and the horse will do as you make him, but you must let him know with your hands, your legs, and your voice."

"How do I do that with my voice?" asked the boy.

"The more you ride, the more your horse will understand you. Maybe a cluck," as she demonstrated making a clucking sound with her tongue, "or a kiss," again she demonstrated with a puckered kiss and its repeated sound, "or something that is easy for you to do. You make the sound as you lean forward, maybe touching him with your heels," she took his heel and pushed it into the ribs of the horse gently, "and lifting the rein." She paused a moment, "You use your whole body to tell him what you want."

Bobcat looked at her, glanced down at the Appy, then said, "C'mon boy," made the clucking sound, leaned forward, and lifted the rein. As the gelding stepped forward, Bobcat beamed and giggled as he left his mother standing and watching. The Appy had been well gentled by the many times Cougar had worked with him at his mother's side and more, and now his gentle spirit showed as he readily stepped out in a smooth walk with the boy in total control. Both Cougar and Gabe watched as the boy and his horse made round after round, and when Bobcat kicked the Appy to a trot, both mom and dad held their breath, but the boy handled it well.

"Next thing you know, they'll be wantin' to go huntin' with us!" declared Ezra as he watched Bobcat as Gabe stood at the fence nearby.

"Yeah, I reckon. Won't that be somethin'?" answered Gabe, grinning.

Dove spoke loud enough for Cougar to hear, "These two are already taking the boys on a hunting trip!"

"And they probably think we'll stay home with the little ones?!" answered Cougar.

Everyone laughed at the thought of the children growing so fast and plans being made long before needed. The younger children had stood at the fence and watched their big brothers ride and both tugged at the fringe of Dove's tunic as they laughed. Fox and Squirrel were about the same age and chimed in together, "Can we ride too?"

Dove dropped to her knees beside the little ones, hugging them both, but answered, "Not today, maybe soon." Chipmunk was past four, Bobcat less than a year younger, and the little ones were just past two, but would be riding soon, just as the older boys had done.

While Ezra and Dove started back to the cabin with the younger ones, Gabe and Cougar took the older boys in hand and let them help strip the tack from the horses. Once finished, they hung up the gear and started to the cabin together. The boys ran ahead, Wolf trotting beside them, and Gabe and Cougar walked arm in arm. Cougar looked to the valley below, saw the remnants of the camp of the Mouache Ute people and said, "It seems so empty with the village gone, but it's peaceful too. I like the quiet," and with a glance to the clear sky, "it's like we have the whole world to ourselves."

"Well, I don't know about the whole world, but at least this part is ours!" declared Gabe, smiling as he leaned his head closer to Cougar's, neither one aware of the eyes that followed their steps as they neared the cabin.

8 / COMPANY

A lone rider followed the deep gulley with the creek as it dropped to the river in the valley bottom, but with the stealth of a predator, he came from the cotton-wood lined draw to round the juniper covered knob and disappear. Once on the flat, he held to the tall sage, until he crossed the river. As he moved from the thick willows and alders, he was met by another scout that came from the mouth of the deep canyon that swallowed the river.

"Ho White Dog!" The greeting caught his attention and he reined up to wait for his fellow scout.

"Little Thunder, what did you find?"

"Deer, coyotes, rabbits . . ." drawled the younger scout. "You?"

"A cabin of a white man and others. They have fine horses and women!"

"No buffalo?"

"Sign, some fresh sign, and there was a village, but no more."

"Perhaps Big Wind will have more," answered Little Thunder.

"The herd moved through here several days past. They could be long gone now," suggested White Dog. The three warriors had been given the task of finding the herd of buffalo the hunting party had followed from the Bayou Salado. It was unusual for the herd to move from the usually fertile park, but the dry winter and spring had put many herds on the move. This valley was further west than their hunting parties usually traveled, putting them in the land of their enemy, the Ute, but their people needed the meat. Other hunting parties had traveled far from their village to other lands and would settle for deer, elk, and antelope, but the people needed the buffalo for more than just the meat. The giant of the plains provided hides for lodges, thick leather for the soles of their moccasins, and every other part of the beast that was used by the people to sustain their way of life.

The rest of the hunting party had stopped in the grassy flat that shouldered the river, giving their horses a bit of rest and graze as they awaited the return of the scouts. Big Wind had already returned and Owl's Tail, the war leader of the *Bäsawunena* tribe of the *Hinono'eiteen* or the Arapaho nation, stood to greet them. Owl's Tail was the headman, and the others of the hunting party were a part of the Greasy Faces band. He had joined this band when he took Blue Cloud, a member of this band, for his wife. It was the custom of the people for the man to join the band of his wife, and Owl's Tail had soon become a respected warrior and leader of the people.

Owl's Tail stepped toward the returning scouts, Big Wind slightly behind him, as he asked for the report from the scouts. Little Thunder spoke first, "The river goes into a great canyon, only deer and coyotes were found."

Owl's Tail nodded, looked to White Dog who reported, "No fresh sign of buffalo, but there is a cabin with a white man, two women that might be Shoshone, four children and another man who looks like a buffalo! They have several fine horses and I saw rifles."

Owl's Tail frowned, "A man that looks like a buffalo?"

White Dog nodded, "His hair, like the buffalo, his color, like the buffalo. He was," White dog lifted his shoulders and flexed his arms to suggest great muscles, "built like a buffalo. But he walked with a stick, his leg was splinted."

Owl's Tail scowled, looking from one scout to the other, then asked White Dog, "Did this white man have a black horse, long mane and tail?" he motioned to his neck to emphasize the long mane.

White Dog frowned, "Yes! He was a fine animal, a stallion!" he answered, wonder showing in his expression as to how his head man could know of this horse. "But how would you know this?"

Owl's Tail let a bit of a grin tug at the corner of his mouth as he lifted one eyebrow, "I might know these men. They visited our village many summers ago, they fought with our warriors against our enemies! If these are the same men, my father, Sitting Elk, gave these men the names of Spirit Bear and Black Buffalo. These men are great warriors!"

"The people of the cabin also had a big black wolf that walked with them and there was sign of a village, but they are gone from there," added White Dog, making a swooping motion with his hand to indicate moving to the north up the long valley.

Owl's Tail turned to Big Wind, "You will go with the others to the place of the buffalo. I will take White Dog, Crooked Nose, and Little Thunder and will go to see these fine horses of this white man."

Gabe and Ezra sat on the porch enjoying their after-supper coffee and watching the dim colors of the eastern sky. It was not uncommon for the setting sun to cast its colors across the wide valley and paint the west faces of the eastern mountains with the faded paints of the evening sunset. Wolf lay between the men as they enjoyed the time when few words passed between them, but the silent communication of life-long friendship held sway.

Wolf lifted his head suddenly as he came to his feet, head down and lip snarling. Ezra grabbed his Lancaster and struggled to his feet to stand leaning against the porch post as Gabe snatched up his Ferguson rifle and leaped from the porch, Wolf at his side as they took to the edge of the trees. Ezra spoke softly through the crack of the door, "Comp'ny comin'! Arm yourselves!" He heard the rustling of the women as they ushered the children into the back bedroom and gathered their weapons to go to the windows. Dove took the window that angled toward the clearing, but Cougar slipped out the back door, preferring to find her own cover and be on the attack rather than try to defend within the walls of the cabin.

Gabe bent and moved side to side, craning to see any movement through the trees. Their cabin was surrounded by thick pines, ponderosa, fir, and spruce, but just below the cabin was a thicket of aspen. The clearing with the cabin offered a good field of fire and Gabe and Wolf were hidden just inside the tree line on the uphill side near the bluff. A narrow trail twisted through the trees to the creek below and angled up to the clearing. It was at this trail that Wolf kept his attention. A low growl rumbled from his chest and Gabe knew the threat was nearing.

Gabe eared back the hammer on the Ferguson rifle,

felt at his waist for his pistol, and slowly lifted the muzzle of the rifle toward the trail. Leaning against the rough bark of the ponderosa, he waited. The wind came off the bluff behind him, carrying his scent toward the trail, but Gabe heard the rattle of hooves on rocks as several horses approached. The horses stopped, but Gabe could tell at least one, maybe more, had dismounted, then two horses continued up the trail. Gabe grinned, knowing the tactic and moved back in the trees. He knew every inch of this land, every trail, every clearing, and could almost identify every tree and the birds that nested in them. With just a moment's thought, he believed he knew where one of the warriors would be found as he tried to flank the others. The terrain allowed but a few possibilities and Gabe moved to a high point where he could see and not be seen.

The clearing and cabin were on a shoulder that lay just below the edge of the long bluff that fronted the upper meadow. With the slope of that shoulder dropping to the valley and the creek bottom, aspen covered most of the slope and as is typical with the quakies of the Rockies, the spindly trees grew thick and close. But Cougar was wily and spry and moved through the thickets as quietly as the evening breeze filtered through the quaking leaves. Movement caught her eye and she stopped, standing as still and yet as supple as the white barked aspen that yielded to the mountain breeze. She saw a warrior, stealthily moving through the trees, a bow with a nocked arrow in his hands as he worked his way toward the clearing and the cabin. Cougar watched and listened, heard the footfalls of two horses on the trail and grinned, knowing this man was trying to flank the clearing on the downhill side of the slope.

The attention of the warrior known as Little Thunder was focused on the edge of the clearing and upon his chosen route through the trees. He picked his steps, moving steadily and quietly, keeping trees between him and the clearing. Cougar followed, also with a nocked arrow in her bow as she held it across her body, timing each footfall with that of the warrior before her. She heard voices come from the clearing and saw the man stop, then carefully move a little closer, probably to get a line of sight on anyone in the clearing. Dove kept pace with the man and when he stopped, she was less than ten yards behind him. She was confident that if he started to shoot into the clearing, she could drop him before he loosed an arrow. She smiled as she leaned against the nearest tree, waiting.

Owl's Tail and White Dog rode slowly into the clearing, Owl's Tail holding his hand high, palm forward, as he spoke, "Yah et tay!" a common greeting among the tribes of the plains. He watched Ezra as he stood, partially shielded by the porch post, his rifle held on Owl's Tail. The war leader continued, "I am Owl's Tail, headman of the *Bäsawunena* tribe of the *Hinono'eiteen,* the Arapaho people. I come in peace."

He spoke in the Algonquian dialect of the plains, and Ezra was surprised to hear the language he learned several years ago when they stayed with the Arapaho people. Ezra answered, "Why are you here?"

The war leader lowered his hand and asked, "Are you called Black Buffalo?"

Ezra frowned, surprised to hear this man use his name, but answered, "I am called Black Buffalo."

"Do you have a friend called Spirit Bear?"

"Yes."

"It was my father, Sitting Elk, that gave you those names when you fought with my people against our enemies."

Ezra frowned as he looked at the man, "I do not remember one known as Owl's Tail."

"I was a young warrior and unproven at the time, but I remember you and Spirit Bear well."

Ezra stepped from behind the post, lowered his rifle and motioned for Owl's Tail to come forward and step down. As the man came near, Ezra suggested, "You might want to call your other men in from the trees before they are killed by Spirit Bear and Cougar Woman."

Owl's tail frowned, then relaxed and made the call of an owl to signal his men. Ezra imitated the call of the night hawk to let Gabe know it was alright to return. When Little Thunder and Crooked Nose stepped into the clearing, they were startled when Gabe and Wolf and Cougar Woman followed them from the trees. But when Ezra explained, smiles spread around, and tensions were relieved. Gabe suggested, "We must have a fire so that we may sit and visit!" and began building a fire in the fire ring that lay near the edge of the clearing, the same fire often used for cooking and more, but would now be a fire of peace talk.

9 / FOREWARNING

In the Comanche village, Many Bears strode from the council, anger flaring as he grumbled his rage and disagreement. It was not the way of the people for arguments to go unsettled, nor was it the way of the council to dictate to any one warrior except in matters of the entire village. Any warrior had the right to gain followers and mount his own war party or hunting party, and those that had proven themselves as leaders that led successful forays against the enemies, easily gained followers eager to join them on their next raid. Crazy Hawk and Rattling Voice followed Many Bears as he went to his lodge and willingly listened as he voiced his complaint.

"We are the *Yaparuhka* of the *Numunuu!* We are warriors! We do not let some white man and his followers tell us how to fight! We do not run from the Ute! They are our enemy! Why does White Knife become like a woman? He let this white man kill my brother and thinks we should not have vengeance!?"

The three men were seated on the blankets beside the cookfire just outside the lodge of Many Bears. Crazy Hawk watched as two women tended the cookfire and the meal, one was the wife of Many Bears, Bear Chaser, the other was the woman of his dead brother, Fox Tail. It was expected of the brother or family members to take the responsibility of caring for the family of a brother who had been killed in battle or on a raid. Many Bears and his woman had two sons, but Fox Tail was pregnant with their first child, and now Many Bears must provide for both lodges. Crazy Hawk glanced from Fox Tail to Many Bears, "Has the woman of your brother asked for the blood of his killers?"

"She does not have to ask! I want the blood of his killers! I want their scalps hanging from my coup stick!"

"Your brother was the one who could make the cry like the big cat of the mountains, and White Knife said it was the woman of the white man who killed him!"

"No woman could kill my brother!" snarled Many Bears, as he looked from Crazy Hawk to Rattling Voice. "You said you killed three Ute warriors, and there were many others. Is this true?"

"I do not lie! I would have stayed to fight, but there were too many!"

"So, it was the Ute warriors from the village that killed my brother?"

"Who else?" asked Rattling Voice, shrugging.

"Then we will mount a war party to get vengeance for our brothers that were killed! The village was large, and we must have many warriors, but the council waits. We cannot wait!" demanded Many Bears. He glared at the two before him and with a swift motion, "Go! Gather the warriors! We will leave at first light to avenge our brothers!"

* * * * *

Owl's Tail and his three men rode into the camp of the Arapaho by the dim light of the big moon that hung in the star-bedecked sky. The cool breeze of early evening held a bit of a chill as it carried the crisp air from the high mountains on the west edge of the wide valley. Big Wind had chosen a campsite at the edge of a small stream overshadowed by the bluff on the south edge. It was one of the many feeder streams that carried snowmelt into the waters of the Arkansa, but offered clear drinking water to the many travelers, man, and beast alike. The war leader stepped down, greeted the others, and asked Big Wind, "Any sighting of the buffalo?"

"The sign is fresh, two, maybe three, days old. There is also sign of a hunt that took several buffalo.

Perhaps the Ute village, before they left."

"Spirit Bear said the Ute have gone north to their summer camp and a camp of other bands. He also said there are Comanche that have raided his horses, but they were killed. Some returned to their people. Spirit Bear said there was a hunting party of three hands, but they did not approach the Ute people as they hunted and took the buffalo. They are the same ones that attacked his lodge and three died."

"Did he say where their village is?" asked Big Wind.

"He did not know; he did not follow. The Comanche were watching from the hills, there," he pointed with his chin to the dark line of hills on the far side of the river.

"If the Comanche have a village, and three hands in just a hunting party, we do not have enough warriors to do battle with them."

"We need the meat from the buffalo," resolved Owl's Tail, dropping to the ground beside the small fire. "If the herd is near, we will take as many as we can carry. We will have scouts far out to give warning if the Comanche come near."

"If our horses are loaded with meat, we cannot outrun the Comanche."

"Then we will fight!"

Big Wind looked from Owl's Tail to the fire and back, "Would Spirit Bear and the others fight with us against the Comanche. You said they had attacked his lodge; they are his enemies!"

"He is but one man. There are children with his women, and his friend, Black Buffalo, cannot ride." He paused, looked around the camp at the other men, then looked at Big Wind, "We will make our prayers to the Creator and the old men for guidance and protection during our hunt. We will leave camp before first light," he declared, nodding to the men as a group to send them to their blankets.

* * * * *

Ezra leaned back in his chair, his bum leg propped on a stool beside the corner of the table, reached for his coffee cup and brought it to his mouth as he spoke to Gabe, "You think them Arapaho might run into the Comanche?"

"Might. But at least the Ute are gone. The Arapaho, Ute, and Comanche are all enemies of one another. I'd hate to think what would happen if all three tribes went after the same buffalo herd. I just imagine there would be more than buffalo blood on the ground."

Ezra thought for a moment, then frowned, "If I remember right, Stone Buffalo said there were some Southern Ute, what'd he call 'em, *Weminuche* I think he said. Didn't he say this was close to their country?"

"Believe he did, ummhmm," answered Gabe, frowning.

"Then it wouldn't be a stretch for us to run into some of 'em up this way after the buffalo. And if things are dry like White Knife said, it might just happen."

"As if we didn't have enough to be worried about!" responded Gabe, shaking his head.

Ezra just grinned and leaned back to sip his coffee. He glanced at Gabe, "So, now what? You gonna try to be a peacemaker or sumpin'?"

Gabe frowned, then looked up at Ezra, "Not a bad idea. But how?"

"Don't look at me! The only way I know to make peace is with my war club. Once I hit someone with that, they become real peaceable like."

"Maybe I should go to their village, talk with the leaders."

"I reckon you're talkin' 'bout the Comanche, but what about the Arapaho? Do you know where either village is?"

"Nope."

"What makes you think they'd listen to you even if you found 'em?"

Gabe frowned, scowled at Ezra, "I dunno."

Ezra chuckled, "You know, since we've been on this journey, we've visited with or fought against about, oh, at least a dozen different tribes, prob'ly more, and ever' one of 'em had bitter enemies livin' nearby. It just seems to be in the nature of folks out thisaway to not get along! You'd think with all this country, they'd learn to live peaceable like, wouldn'tchu think?"

Gabe looked at his friend, cocked his head to the side, "You know, that's quite a mouthful you just spouted, but for the life of me, I can't disagree with what you said."

"Then maybe we oughta leave well enough alone. If the fight comes to us, well then, we get involved, but these folks have been fightin' for longer'n both of us have been alive, so, I say, just leave 'em be!"

Gabe chuckled, looked around the table at a grinning Dove and Cougar, and condescended, "I reckon you're right!"

10 / WAR PARTY

The party of warriors assembled at the lodge of Many Bears before first light. When Many Bears stepped from the hide cover tipi, he stood before the anxious warriors, but was disappointed by the number. His first glance showed about twelve warriors, most young, many unproven, but all anxious. The only experienced warriors were Crazy Hawk and Rattling Voice, but as he reached for the rein of his mount, another rode up to join them. Many Bears grinned when he saw the respected warrior, Wears no Shoes. The man had ridden on many raids and war parties, always gaining honors and respect from the men of the *Yaparuhka* Comanche. Many Bears motioned for Wears no Shoes to join him at the head of the raiders, a quick glance showing Crazy Hawk felt slighted, but backed away.

"We go to gain vengeance on our enemy, the Ute people. They and their friends, the white man, and his people, killed our brothers and must pay with their blood!" shouted Many Bears as he swung up astride of his mount. The horse was a blue roan, dark legs, mane, and tail, and he pranced with excitement and anticipation. Many Bears had painted the horse with hand prints on his chest, lightning bolts down his legs, and the emblem of the sun on his shoulders. This was Many Bears favorite hunting and war pony, and he dug his heels into the horse's ribs to lunge forward and lead the war party.

The men were painted for war with the preferred colors of black for death, and red for blood prominent among them. Many Bears had painted the lower half of his face black, the top white, and red streaks coming from his eyes to his chin. Others had painted their faces with the familiar patterns used during battles, some with designs, or emblems, others with their face completely painted in one or two colors, but all with the thought of striking terror in the hearts of their enemy. Wears no Shoes had painted his face with two colors, divided down the middle from his forehead to his chin, red on one side, yellow on the other, no highlights or designs. This was the pattern he always used and was readily recognized, even by enemies faced before.

They crossed the river and followed the same trail used by White Knife on his return from the fight with the white man. The trail shouldered the river through the narrow valley, and the sky was fading to grey when they broke into the open of the wide valley with the buffalo herd. Many Bears lifted his hand to stop the men, motioned for two to come forward, "You, Crazy Hawk, there," he pointed to a high bluff at the end of a long ridge on the north side of the valley. He turned toward the second man, "You, Walks Alone, there!" pointing to a similar bluff on the south edge. The men knew what was expected and immediately set their horses to the bluffs. Many Bears motioned to the others to step down, water their horses in the shallows at river's edge, as they waited for the scouts' reports.

Crazy Hawk tethered his mount to a juniper, struggled up the steep slope, and bellied down to search the valley. The grey light of early morning was fast fading to a pale blue, a clear sky with just a couple clouds that caught the pink of the rising sun on their bellies, offered Crazy Hawk ample light to search the wide valley. In the distance on the southwest end, the buffalo herd lay like a rumply brown blanket over the green of the valley floor. He shaded his eyes as he scanned the upper end of the valley, the area where the Ute were reported to have their village, but he saw nothing. As he started to turn away, a wisp of a dust cloud showed near the ridges of foothills that pushed into the valley floor, and he focused his attention on the dust. With squinted eyes, he followed the movement, recognizing riders, several, maybe three hands or more. He watched for a moment, realized they were headed for the buffalo, then rose to return with his report.

Walks Alone was unable to see the southern end of the valley, a long ridge and shoulder from the foothills pushed into the valley from the south and beginning of the Sangre de Cristo mountains. He did see the dust cloud and also guessed there were about three hands of riders, but they were riding toward the southwest end of the valley. He quickly rose and descended the bluff, stepped aboard his bay and white paint gelding to return to the others and report.

"Three hands of riders," began Crazy Hawk, pointing back to the far side of the valley, "moving toward the herd of buffalo."

"Ute?" asked Many Bears.

"Too far, I could not tell. But the Ute already had a buffalo hunt, why go again?"

Many Bears frowned, mumbled something, then looked to Walks Alone for his report. "I saw the riders. I could not tell who they were, I could not see the buffalo."

Many Bears looked at Wears no Shoes, "It would be better to fight three hands of hunters than the whole village!" He had not asked the question, but still expected Wears to answer, but the seasoned warrior just nodded.

"Then we will go!" He looked at Crazy Hawk, "You," and to Walks Alone, "and you, scout ahead!"

The two men turned their mounts to the south end of the valley and took off at a canter. With the south end of the valley lying between the main branch of the Arkansa river, and the smaller fork that came from the mountains to the west, this was the more fertile end of the valley and they were not concerned with raising a dust cloud that would give away their presence. Crazy Hawk had mentally marked where the hunters were and the direction of their travel and used the landmarks to guide their movements. He kept his horse at a canter, Walks Alone staying alongside, and quickly covered the stretch that took them around the pointed bluff and nearer the smaller river.

To his left, the south flank of the wide valley, the foothills climbed steadily rising timbered slopes to the crest of the upper end of the Sangre de Cristo mountains. On his right, Crazy Hawk and Walks Alone were sheltered by the thick cottonwoods that rode the banks of the smaller fork of the Arkansa river. Beyond the smaller stream, the wide fertile green flats were bordered by the continuous bluff of a long mesa that stretched into the bowels of the valley and the buffalo herd grazed contentedly on the lush grasses of the flats. With the bluff on one side, the small river on the other, the animals were well concealed from the usual four-legged hunter, but man has a way of searching out his prey, unlike other predators, and the dust cloud atop the long mesa told of the approaching hunters.

Crazy Hawk signaled to Walks Alone to move into the cottonwoods by the stream and followed him into the trees. As they stepped down, Hawk spoke, "The hunting party is up there," pointing with his chin to the mesa, "they will approach the buffalo soon. You tell Many Bears what we have seen, I will wait and watch." Walks Alone nodded, swung back aboard his dun gelding, and started back with his report, keeping near the trees to avoid being seen.

Big Wind, of the Arapaho hunters, rode back to Owl's Tail and the others as they crested the long mesa. With a raised hand, he stopped before the leader of the party, "The buffalo herd is there," twisting around to motion to the south rim of the mesa, "in a long valley. This mesa gives us a good view of the herd."

"It is good," responded Owls Tail, lifting his eyes to the rising sun that was showing its brilliance at the far end of the valley. The golden orb seemed to come from the belly of the earth as it nestled in the notch that was the mouth of the canyon holding the Arkansa river. "The Creator smiles on us. He has gifted us with a good day, a great herd, and good

hunters. We will have a good hunt!" he declared as he
gigged his mount forward. He kicked his horse to a
canter, anxious to get to the herd and plan their hunt,
while in his mind was the image of the Comanche
and what might happen if the Comanche found them
busy at the kill of many buffalo. It would be hard
to defend against an enemy attack, but they must
have meat, or the village would go hungry, his family
would go hungry.

He reined up well back from the edge of the mesa
bluff, motioned for his men to step down and pointed
out two hunters to hold the many horses. With hand
signals, he directed the others to fan out and follow
him to the edge to observe the buffalo. As they neared,
Owls Tail dropped to all fours, then bellied down
to go to the edge. Below them, the massive herd of
buffalo covered the greenery of the valley floor like
a thick woolen blanket. The occasional rumble and
snorts of the beasts, the clatter of their hooves and
horns, was the undercurrent of the brown tide that
shifted and moved across the wide valley floor. At
its widest point, from the bluff of the long mesa to
the edge of the small river the valley was just over a
mile, and the length of the valley stretched along the
tips of the many finger ridges for over ten miles, but
the herd was bunched in a stretch of about one mile
by three miles. In places the beasts were clustered so
thick, not a blade of greenery could be seen, yet at the

edges, big bulls rolled in dust wallows to rid themselves of pesky bugs. Buffalo birds rode the backs of many bison, some with eight or ten birds, picking off pesky parasites.

It was a serene image, but the Arapaho hunters did not come for scenery, but for meat. Owls Tail motioned Big Wind and Crooked Nose near, "You," nodding to the two, "take one hand of men with you, go there," he pointed to the lower part of the valley below the herd, "circle the east end. I will take the others to the upper end, spread across the valley. We will strike first. When you hear us begin, you start. The buffalo will be confused and mill around. We will take many, but only what we can take away." He paused and motioned to the others, "Little Thunder and Creeping Bear will scout below you and across the stream for Comanche."

"It is good," stated Big Wind, glancing to Crooked Nose who nodded agreement.

"Then go!" declared Owls Tail as he motioned the others to mount up. He started west along the edge of the bluff, occasionally moving closer to the edge to view the herd, and when he was above the animals, he pointed his mount through the trees that clung to the side of the bluff to work his way to the valley floor. He reined up at the edge of the trees, spoke softly to the men, "Ready your weapons. I will lead us across the valley, stretch out and be ready to move into the herd as one." The others nodded as the few with rifles checked their loads, while the others nocked arrows, and hefted lances. At Owls Tail's signal, they started from the trees, holding their mounts to a steady walk, but the animals were anxious for the hunt and several pranced sideways as they moved, necks arched with the force of their riders holding the reins taut. It was about to begin.

11 / SCOUT

A big bull rolled in the dust bowl, came to his feet, and was surprised to see the riders coming toward him. He lowered his head and pawed at the dirt, snorted, and shook his head, threatening those that would come near the herd. The riders came on without wavering their pace, watching the bull and the other nearby buffalo. The bull danced his rear around, keeping his face to the perceived threat, snorted and took two threatening steps forward. When the riders continued, the bull lost interest, and strolled back to the herd. A big cow stepped between the riders and her pale orange calf, letting the calf butt her bag and nurse, but watching the riders. The other buffalo near the riders paid little attention, continuing to graze, occasionally snort, and lift their heads, chewing on the mouthful of grass.

At Owls Tail's nod, the six men spaced out along

the upper part of the meadow, Stands on Clouds anchoring the line, each picking their targets as they sat idle, watching the others move further toward the little river that served as a barrier to the herd. Owls Tail stopped, motioned to White Dog and Little Raven to continue and space out as the others. As each hunter stopped, they readied their weapons and turned to face the herd. With a glance to Stands on Clouds on his left, then to White Dog on the far right, Owls Tail lifted his bow high in the air to swing the weapon overhead and drop it forward.

The hunters dug heels to their mounts and charged into the herd, eyes on their chosen prey. Stands on Clouds was the first to send an arrow into the lone cow, who just lifted her head and watched as the hunter neared, but when the arrow plunged into her chest she lunged forward and within two steps was at a full run, the feathered fletching fluttering in the wind. Stands Alone quickly nocked another arrow as he guided his mount with leg pressure, swinging around to give chase. At a glance, he spotted White Dog lying low on the neck of his horse, readying his lance, but Stands Alone was nearing the lumbering cow. He brought his bow to full draw, moved his mount closer to the cow and sent the arrow to drive deep into her chest. The cow was slobbering blood and snot, she bellowed once, stumbled, and dropped her head into the dirt, cartwheeling end over end.

White Dog sided a young bull that just started walking, but when the rider came close, the bull moved to the lumbering gait of the big beasts. White Dog quickly drew close and at the last instant, instead of throwing his lance, chose to drive it deep into the side of the bull. The impact of the sharp bladed point and the power of the thrust drove the lance deep into the chest, just behind the front leg. The impact drove the bull to stumble to the side, and White Dog turned his horse away. The bull stumbled again, stopped, shook his head, and tried to take another step, but his legs gave way and he dropped on his chin to roll to his side. White Dog retrieved his bow from over his shoulder, slowly came near the big bull as he nocked an arrow, and brought the bow to full draw, but it was evident the bull was dead. White Dog looked around, searching for another target, but the herd had moved away from the initial attack.

On the east end of the herd, Big Wind and Crooked Nose saw the beasts start to move and knew the others had begun their assault. Big Wind waved his arm high to Crooked Nose and the others between them to start their surge into the herd. They moved like a sidewinder into the mass of animals, picking their targets. Crooked Nose was the first to score a hit, but he had to stay after the young bull and with three arrows in its neck and chest, the bull finally staggered and fell.

Walks Alone rode toward the rest of the Comanche war party at a canter, swung around to side the leader, Many Bears, "The hunters are coming across the flat," he pointed across the valley to the long mesa beyond, "the buffalo are in the bottom, across this river," motioning to the small cottonwood lined river beside the trail. "Crazy Hawk waits in the trees near the herd!"

"How many hunters?" asked Many Bears.

"Three hands!"

Many Bears nodded, looked at Wears no Shoes, "We will go to the trees, then plan our attack."

"We can wait until they make their kill, even wait until they butcher. They will be tired, no cover, easy to kill," drawled Wears no Shoes.

Many Bears nodded, pointed with his chin to the trees and motioned Walks Alone to lead the way to where Crazy Hawk waited.

The Arapaho scout, Creeping Bear motioned to Little Thunder to take to the trees beside the river, while he would move closer to the east end of the long meadow that held the buffalo. With a nod, Little Thunder kicked his mount to a canter and headed for the trees. With little cover, he kept to the low end with the thickets of berry bushes and willows, but once at the tree line of the little river, he moved into the thicker cottonwoods and alders, taking cover near the shaded bank. He tethered his mount and moved to the water's edge, finding an observation point that revealed the opposite shore and the flats beyond. As he stepped to the edge of the willows, the sound of hoofbeats rose above the chuckling of the water and prompted him to drop back. As he pushed the thin branches of the willow aside, he saw a warrior stretching out on his pony, moving downstream to the broader expanse of the valley. *He is in a hurry, perhaps he is a scout, he and his horse are painted for war!* thought Little Thunder, but the thought of a scout, made him more wary, knowing it was probable there was another scout left to watch.

Within moments of seeing the rider, Little Thunder spotted the tethered and painted horse of a second scout and soon saw the man sitting on the fork of a cottonwood about fifteen feet off the ground. As Little Thunder watched, he saw the man was painted for war also, and watched as he shaded his eyes to look at the buffalo herd, but if it was the herd that interested him, why the lofty perch? Little Thunder backed away, stealthily made his way back to his mount and started out to find Creeping Bear.

"Two scouts, Comanche! Painted for war! One left," pointing down stream and into the bigger end of the valley, "in a hurry. I think he is going for other warriors! That one," pointing with his chin to the river, "is in a tree, watching the herd and our warriors!

You should go to Owls Tail and warn him!"

"Comanche? Painted for war?" he asked, "But you saw only two scouts?"

Little Thunder nodded curtly, "But the one was going for more warriors!"

Creeping Bear nodded, paused as he looked in the direction of the scout and to the lower end of the valley, "I will go. But I must act like there is nothing wrong so that scout will not warn the others."

"Yes, but you will see Big Wind and Crooked nose first, tell them, but hurry to Owls Tail! I will return to the river and watch for the others!"

While behind cover, Creeping Bear moved as fast as possible, but when he broke from the brush, the hunt was already on and Big Wind and the others were in the midst of the herd. He made the choice to use the herd for cover and ride as fast as possible to give the message to Owls Tail. Within moments, he saw the downed buffalo of the hunters on the upper end and kicked his horse to a run to find Owls Tail and came to a stop when he spotted their war leader beside the carcass of a big buffalo.

"Comanche! Little Thunder saw their scouts, there is one in the trees behind you by the river watching now. Another rode fast downstream probably going for others. They are painted for war!" shouted Creeping Bear, desperate to be herd over the sounds of the buffalo. The big herd was milling about, disturbed by the killing, the smell of blood, and hunters all around. The snorts, bellows, grunts, clatter of hooves on rocks and horns clashing against one another, was like an undercurrent of low thunder. The dust from thick coats rolled in dirt and the shuffling of the thousands of hooves had turned the green meadow into a low lying dust cloud, offering cover to the hunters.

Owls Tail looked for the others, spotted most of those that were with him and turned to Creeping Bear, "Go, tell the others, two to a carcass and be ready for attack. Work on the carcass like usual, but one watch, one work. Those on the far end are to come close here! Go tell Big Wind and the others with him to come this way, act like they are helping butcher, but come close!"

Creeping Bear waited for more, but Owls Tail barked, "Go!"

Walks Alone led the Comanche war party to the waiting Crazy Hawk who spotted them and came from his perch to greet the others. When Many Bears rode up, Crazy Hawk stepped aside as the leader stepped down, "The hunters are Arapaho!" he declared. "They split their number," he pointed to the west end, "seven, others at the bottom."

"Arapaho!" spat Many Bears, turning toward Wears no Shoes, "They are our enemy!"

"We came for the Ute! You said the Ute killed our

brothers; we are here for vengeance!" growled Wears
no Shoes, but loud enough for the others to hear.

"We are Comanche!" retorted Many Bears, "We kill
our enemy where we find them!" His lip curled in
a snarl; Many Bears glared at the others still sitting
their mounts. Several of the waiting warriors lifted
their weapons in the air but were stifled from shouting their war cry by the uplifted hand of Many Bears.
He motioned the men down, and spoke to Wears no
Shoes, "Let us look at the enemy!" and motioned to
the riverbank.

The two leaders pushed through the willows and
bushes on the bank of the little river, working their
way to a point that offered a view of the far meadow.
With thick cover on the far side, Many Bears waded
into the water, Wears no Shoes close behind, and
picked their way through the brush to see the meadow and the milling herd of buffalo. As they watched,
several riders pushed through the herd, moving to the
upper end of the meadow where the rest of the hunters
were busy with downed carcasses. Many Bears and
Wears no Shoes worked their way closer, kept to the
brush, and watched as the rest of the hunters joined
the first group at the butchering tasks. Bears turned
to Wears no Shoes, "We come from there," pointing
to the upper end of the meadow where the grass was
untouched and the area unhindered with brush or
other obstacles. "We will be upon them before they

get to their weapons! The buffalo will also be ours and their horses will carry the meat to our people!"

"What about the vengeance?" asked Wears no Shoes.

"We can go after the Ute after we feast on the buffalo!" declared a confident Many Bears.

12 / SKIRMISH

The Comanche war party rode west, keeping the cottonwoods along the river between them and the Arapaho who were busy at the butchering of the downed buffalo. As the river crowded against the trees that draped the flank of the taller timbered foothills, Many Bears led his men across the shallow river and into the scattered trees that marked the west end of the long meadow. At Many Bears nod, Wears no Shoes led half of the warriors toward the low bluff that shouldered the big, long mesa while Many Bears and his men waited in the trees.

As Wears no Shoes and his men disappeared over the slight knoll, Many Bears motioned his men to spread out and start forward. A slight rise had kept them from view until about seventy yards from the first of the Arapaho busy at the butchering. The instant they came in view, Many Bears glanced down the line at his men, raised his lance high and screamed his war cry. The line lunged forward, horses digging hooves in the dirt, warriors screaming, the band covering the distance in brief moments. Several stood in their stirrups, drawing their bows, others lifted their lances or war clubs and screamed as they neared the Arapaho.

Owls Tail had stationed a scout near the river, well hidden in the trees and at first sight of the Comanche, he gave the shrill chirping of an osprey in warning. The signal was quickly passed, and every warrior pulled his weapons close, scanning the flats before them, choosing their point of cover. When the first war cry sounded, every man dropped to a knee, using the carcass of the buffalo for cover, some lifting the big head to rest on the body, offering additional cover. As the Comanche charged, the Arapaho waited until the last moment, then sent a hail of arrows into the charging horde. Many feathered shafts fluttered through the air and several found their targets. Two of the Comanche tumbled backwards off their horses, another slumped forward on his horse's neck, grabbing a fist full of mane to stay astride the charging war pony.

As the hail of arrows whispered overhead, the Comanche let fly with their own. The sky was streaked with the crisscrossing shafts, and only one shaft struck an Arapaho hidden behind a pile of meat and bones. The arrow drove into the shoulder of Shoots a Lot, just after he loosed his own arrow. After the first hail of arrows, the Arapaho readied another, but most were ducking and dodging war clubs and lances, and White Dog was knocked to the side by a glancing blow of a war club in the hand of a screaming Comanche Crazy Hawk.

The Comanche charged past the dodging and scampering Arapaho, intent on turning their mounts for another charge, and to join with Wears no Shoes and his men to rally for the second assault. But they were in the thick of the herd of buffalo. The screaming of war cries, the shooting of the few firearms, and the running horses, together with the sudden activity and pandemonium, all combined to spook the herd into a stampede. As the big beasts lunged together to flee from the commotion, two of the Comanche horses stumbled and fell, sending their riders tumbling into the path of the stampede. Many Bears looked around, fear showing in his wide eyes, as he screamed to his men, "The river! Ride to the river!" and pulled hard on the reins of his mount, shouldering against a big cow that was protecting her calf on the far side. The panicked buffalo tossed her head back, trying to hook the horse on her horns but only succeeded in making the horse rear up to escape the thrust. Many Bears grabbed handfuls of mane, clutched tightly with his legs and held on as the big blue roan fought for footing. The gelding came down on all fours and pushed through the herd, using the momentum of the beasts to work his way to the riverbank and the heavy trees for cover.

Others fought against the brown tide, knowing their horses could not force their way they used the movement and better footing of their war ponies that were also experienced at buffalo hunting, to wend their way through the mass. Many Bears had found safety in the tall cottonwoods and dropped to the ground, letting his mount go to the water to drink. The Comanche leader kept to the big trees, watching as several of his men fought their way free and made for the cover of the trees.

As the herd thundered past, the dust rose, dirt clods flew, the ground rumbled beneath them and the bellowing, snorting, beasts made the fierce Comanche warriors suck wind as they fought to still their hearts from fright of their narrow escape. As the roar of the stampede subsided, dust began to settle, and the Comanche came from the trees, they sought not for an enemy, but a friend and fellow warrior. Many Bears motioned several to join him, as others searched for their friends and brothers. As they gathered, each man gave his report, "Two fell in the way of the Buffalo, trampled," came the first report.

"Two took arrows in the assault," came another.

"One was struck with an arrow but fell when a big bull gored his horse."

Wears no Shoes rode into the cover with the others, slipped to the ground and with a nod asked the question of Many Bears. The leader dropped his eyes, grumbled, then said, "Five, one hand, of warriors. Three by the buffalo, two by the Arapaho!"

"There is no vengeance in this!" answered the older leader, scowling at Many Bears.

When the charging Comanche rode past, Owls Tail ordered the men to take to the other side of the carcasses, to prepare for another assault, but the assault never came. Owls Tail stood, watching the buffalo herd stampede further away, leaving the churned soil and lingering dust in the air. He searched for the Comanche, motioning his men to stay behind cover. As he watched, he saw a few riders at the edge of the trees by the river's edge some distance away, but there was nothing to indicate another charge. Owls Tail called to Little Raven, "Go! Get the horses!" The young warrior took off at a run, going to the trees near the river where the horses had been tethered at the first sign of an impending attack. Although Owls Tail knew it might be a giveaway that they expected an attack, he preferred the animals to be secured and safe.

Big Wind had sent their horses to the trees below the bluff and now motioned to the young warrior to bring them. With only one man wounded, Shoots a Lot, the youngest warrior of the Arapaho was left to tend to him as the others mounted, readying to meet another charge from the Comanche. Owls Tail mustered the band together, "We will go after the Comanche! They lost two warriors, maybe more in the stampede. The Creator had protected us."

Owls Tail lined out his warriors, five abreast, with Big Wind and White Dog on either side of him and the others staggered in two lines behind them. They followed the churned earth of the stampede, passed the three bodies of the downed Comanche, all trampled and mangled, driven into the dirt by the many monstrous beasts that passed over. As they neared the edge of the trees where the Comanche had been spotted, Owls Tail reined up and called out, "HO! Comanche! I am Owls Tail, headman of the *Bäsawunena* tribe of the *Hinono'eiteen,* the Arapaho people." Owls Tail sat quietly, waiting for a response from the Comanche.

Two men stepped from the trees, the younger one spoke, "I am Many Bears of the *Yaparuhka* band of the *Numunuu* people, what you call Comanche!" Many Bears spoke in the language of the Comanche, but Wears no Shoes stood beside him and translated into the tongue of the Arapaho along with his use of sign language.

Owls Tail spoke, "You have lost many warriors, they fought bravely. We will return to our task of gathering the meat. We give you, your warriors and two," holding up two fingers, "buffalo. It is not our way to use the animals of the great Creator to fight for us. If you want to go to your village, let it be so. If you want to fight, we will do that also!"

Many Bears listened to the translation from Wears no Shoes, although he understood most of what was said by sign. He glowered at the Arapaho leader, turned to Wears no Shoes, but the expression of the older warrior stayed his retort, and with a heavy sigh, he turned back to face Owls Tail. "We will gather our warriors and leave."

Owls Tail nodded, "It is good." He glanced to Big Wind and to White Dog, motioned to the others and the group backed away from the trees, then turned and rode to the carcasses. Although the agreement had been made, Owls Tail said to Big Wind, "Put two scouts on guard, the others will bundle the meat to leave. We will lead our horses until we can make travois. We cannot stay any longer."

The sun was withdrawing its long lances of gold into the folds of darkness behind the western mountains when the Arapaho led their horses from the long meadow. The receding light of dusk saw the hunters and their heavy-laden horses make camp in the upper reaches of a long draw that stretched between two narrow finger ridges that came from the tall granite peaks of the Sawatch range. Come first light, Owls

Tail expected to find some lodgepole pine to make travois to carry the meat, and if not, they would make do with aspen saplings. Tomorrow would see the beginning of their return trip to the Bayou Salado, and perhaps a short visit with Spirit Bear, he should know about the Comanche.

13 / REPORT

"The leader was Many Bears. An older and wiser warrior who knew our language kept the leader from the fight. I think this man will try to do more and I thought it best for you to know," stated Owls Tail. "We must take the meat of the buffalo to our people or we would stay and fight with you."

"So, you think he'll come after us?" asked Gabe, glancing to Ezra. The two men sat on the porch as Owls Tail spoke. He and Crooked Nose sat astride their mounts as they told of the conflict with the Comanche.

"He is a man with much anger. I believe he was on a vengeance quest and thought we were part of the fight his people had when they came after your horses. He is not one to easily back off from his purpose."

Gabe glanced to Ezra and back to Owls Tail, "Well, my friend, we are grateful you told us about this man.

We will prepare and trust our God to protect us."

"It is good. Perhaps one day we will meet again," responded Owls Tail as he reined his mount around to return to his hunting party. With a wave over his shoulder, he and Crooked Nose disappeared into the trees, following the trail from the long arroyo to join his men.

Gabe looked at Ezra, "What'chu think?"

"I think we need to make ready. Apparently the one you let return to his people, White Knife, wasn't it? I reckon he wasn't very convincing."

"The way Owls Tail talked about that leader, Many Bears, sounded like he was a mean one. Maybe he's out for vengeance, might be one o' them that was killed was special to him somehow," suggested Gabe.

"Could be. Or he could just be a mean'un, out for blood. You know how some o'them renegades are, just wanna fight somebody, anybody. That's how they get to be somebody special!" proclaimed Ezra, then frowning he added, "Why does it have to be that way? It ain't just the natives that're like that. We've found people like that ever'where we been. White folks, black folks like them Maroons, Frenchies, Spanish. It shouldn't oughta be that way, but it is."

"Isn't that what the Bible talks about when it says *All have sinned and come short of the glory of God?*"

"Yeah, that's what my pappy always said, 'Man is born to sin and in sin he will die, unless he learns about the blessed Savior! And it's our responsibility to tell them about Jesus!' Then he'd pound on that pulpit and stare down anybody what dared to squirm in their seats! Oh, he's a wonder, he is, yessiree!" Ezra grinned at the remembrance, chuckling and slowly shaking his head.

"I remember. I heard him a time or two, when we used to sneak in the back and hide in the balcony," responded Gabe, grinning just like his friend.

The men sat silent a while, their minds traveling the long roads of memories and families, times long past and probably never to be revisited. Cougar Woman stepped through the door, coffee pot in hand and refilled the men's cups. Dove joined them, whispering as she slowly shut the door, "They're almost asleep." She moved Ezra's crutch aside and sat beside her man as Cougar sat down the pot and joined Gabe, scooting her rocking chair close beside his as she smiled at her man.

"So, what did Owls Tail have to say?" asked Cougar, looking sidelong at Gabe.

"Oh, just that they had a little trouble with some Comanche."

Cougar frowned, "And?"

Gabe chuckled, grinning as he looked at Cougar over the steam rising from his cup, "And he thinks the leader of the Comanche might be trouble for us too."

Cougar's brow wrinkled as she looked at Gabe, "I

thought White Knife would talk peace."

"Ummhmm. But the leader was some firebrand name o' Many Bears. Owls Tail said Many Bears wanted to continue the fight, but an older and wiser warrior kept him back. The Comanche lost five warriors, the Arapaho just had one wounded and outnumbered the other Comanche, so, they agreed to leave. But, Owls Tail said the leader was not happy about it."

Cougar looked down, and as she considered what she learned, she looked all around the clearing before the cabin, the trail that led through the trees to the lower end of the long arroyo and the bluff behind the cabin that bordered the upper meadows where the horses were kept, and more. Her ways of thinking as a war leader of her people coming to the fore as she considered all possibilities. She also knew her man, Spirit Bear, would be thinking in much the same fashion and she also knew they were much alike and preferred to take the fight to their enemy, not wait and try to defend behind the walls of a cabin.

Ezra broke the silence, "I know what you're thinkin'!" as he looked at Gabe and glanced to Cougar Woman.

Gabe let a slow grin split his face as he looked at his friend, "And what am I thinkin'?"

"That you don't want to try to defend the place, and you'd rather take the fight to them!"

"Pretty much, yeah." He looked around, "With the horse herd up yonder, the young'uns, hereabouts, and the limitations on defense, yeah, I'd rather take it to 'em."

Ezra slapped his leg, grimaced, and growled, "But I can't ride, and wouldn't be much help."

"If I tied you to your saddle, gave you your war club and a couple pistols, you'd be more than five or six others, but . . ."

"Yeah, but! But you've got other ideas. I can tell by the look in your eyes, you've already had the fight and whipped 'em all, in your mind anyway."

Gabe grinned, glanced at Cougar Woman and back at Ezra, "Not quite, but I've given it some thought." He paused, nodded toward the arroyo below the cabin, "We've hunted from here to the river, both sides of that creek, and most of the country of this entire valley. I know it pretty well, know most of the places animals would hide out and such. So, I reckon I could cover quite a bit o' country, maybe set some traps, pitfalls, and such, you know, like we done before. And set up an ambuscade or two, make 'em good an' mad. Pick 'em off one or two at a time. Convince 'em it's not a good idea to come after us."

"And when do we start this?" asked Cougar Woman, stoically.

"We?" asked Gabe, frowning. "Woman, you have children to take care of, you know, Bobcat and the little one, what's his name!"

"It is the custom of my people that the sister and brother take care of the children while we," motioning to Gabe and herself, "protect the village." She scowled, "And you know what's his name! Remember, you want to give both our sons white man's names, Gabriel and Boettcher."

Ezra frowned, "You gonna do that?" as he looked at Gabe, scowling.

Gabe snorted, laughed, "Yeah, I thought about it. Nothin' wrong with havin' names like my family and her family too!"

"Hmmm, you got a point there," replied Ezra as he turned to look at Dove. "What do you think, Dove?" Grey Dove smiled but said nothing as she looked from Ezra to Gabe and Cougar and back to Ezra.

Ezra shook his head, looked to Gabe, "See, I can never win an argument with her, she just don't fight fair!"

"She didn't say nothin'!" declared Gabe, slightly confused.

"That's what I mean! You can't argue with nothin'!" responded an exasperated Ezra, shaking his head.

Gabe chuckled, looked at Cougar, "Well, if you're determined, I reckon we better get some things ready for this jaunt."

14 / AMBUSH

Wolf led the way from the cabin, Gabe and Cougar following close behind with the big grey packhorse on a lead behind Gabe. They knew they had the advantage over any attacking force in almost every way but numbers. The Arkansa valley was more like two valleys here below the Sawatch range. The upper and lower ends were open, flat, fertile with deep grasses and more. Between the two was a stretch of finger ridges and dry land abundant with sage, grease brush, rabbit brush and cacti. The larger lower end held the terminus of the Sawatch range and the beginning of the Sangre de Cristos, two mountain ranges that bordered the lush valley on the west and south.

They turned south away from the arroyo and took to a higher butte for Gabe's first survey of the land. An ancient trail took them at an angle up the bluff of the long mesa and Gabe and Cougar stepped down and Gabe dug in the saddle bags for his scope. Cougar asked, "What do you think they will do?"

Gabe paused, pulled out the scope and turned toward the valley. "I'm not sure, but I reckon they'll stay close to the river, except that stretch yonder," pointing to the timbered hillocks and foothills that offered the river an escape from the valley, "the river runs into a long canyon there and there's no trails. So, if I was leadin' a pack of blood thirsty warriors, I'd come up that open rise there," pointing to the flats that stretched between the finger ridges from the mountains behind them and the foothills by the river. "There's plenty of draws and bluffs to offer cover and they could take to these hills and ridges," pointing to the timbered terrain that lay like a dark cape at the edge of the mountains, "and follow any number of trails that would bring them to the cabin." He paused and looked at the wide valley, long shadows stretching from the lowering sun, "Or, they could follow the river, then come up the arroyo to the valley of the white cliffs and our cabin."

Cougar looked at the lay of the land, shading her eyes as she followed the tree line on the west edge of the valley, then turning to look along the river with its green banks made so by berry bushes, alders, willows, and cottonwoods. "I would stay near the river. From there it is easy to see the cliffs," motioning to the chalk like cliffs that shouldered the majestic mountain behind them, "and if the one Comanche that ran is with them, he will tell them of the cliffs that are near our cabin and the meadow with the horses."

Gabe looked at the wide valley again, considering the thoughts of his woman, the experienced war leader. As he looked at the east side of the valley, he tried to imagine the thoughts or tactics the Comanche might take, and remembered, "Those hills yonder *are* where the Comanche were spotted during the buffalo hunt." He paused, then added, "You're prob'ly right. We'll focus our doin's on that side, but we will still need to keep watch up this direction too." He motioned to Wolf and the two started to the point to take advantage of the failing light before the sun dropped behind the mountains.

He sat down, brought up his knees and slipped the scope from its case, stretched it out and focused it on the far side of the valley, just over a mile distant. While Wolf lay belly down at his side, Gabe scanned the edge of the trees on the low rising hills moving right to left until the hills gave way to the river. Then keeping his scope on the bank of the river and the thicker cottonwoods, he searched the greenery for any movement or sign of life. He spotted some bighorns on the far bank, several deer in the trees and willows, a pair of coyotes, but no horses or warriors. Another scan, slower this time and covering the ground closer in as well as the riverbanks, showed nothing but an abundance of game.

He twisted around to look at the tree line of the flanks of the big mountains, spotted some elk, a big bull moose wading in a small feeder creek below some aspen, and nothing more. With another quick scan, he contracted the scope, cased it, and stood to return to Cougar's side. As he neared, "I reckon we'll camp yonder, nearer the river. There's a wide rift with a little creek runnin' into the river. We can make camp at the bottom of a bluff, plenty of cover."

Cougar nodded, handed him the reins and lead, swung aboard her appaloosa, and waited as Gabe put away the scope and mounted. With a motion to Wolf to lead the way, they dropped off the gentle slope on the south side of the mesa to follow the wide gulch across the open valley before turning south toward the rift. The sun was sending its long shafts of bright gold and orange from behind the shadowed mountain peaks, lending a golden cast to the west faces of the eastern hills and a blanket of pale gold that lay across the valley, as the two riders came to the bluff at the edge of the rift.

* * * * *

"You have failed! You are the cause of the mourning in the lodges on this night! Wears no Shoes told of your attack on the Arapaho and your failure. Instead of honor and vengeance, you brought more death and mourning to our village and the families of our warriors. You went for vengeance when the council had spoken for peace. You and those that would follow you have brought shame on the *Numunuu* people! If you go again for vengeance, it will not be as a leader!" The declaration came from Old Owl, the headman of the village and the father of White Knife. He stood before Many Bears, his arms across his chest, and as he finished his declaration, he turned his back on the disgraced warrior. The other council members who had sat quietly during the pronouncement, stood, and turned their back to Many Bears.

The declaration of the council was a rare action on the part of the leaders of the Comanche and most other people of the plains, for every warrior has the right to make his own choices and if others choose to follow him, it is not the say of the council to forbid it. But if the council speaks, it is for the safety and security of the village and then their declarations are binding on all members of the village. Many Bears had chosen to go against what he knew was the will of the council, and it was not the first time the strong-willed man had taken his own path against the will of the people, but it was to be the last. Many Bears stood, stubbornly proud, and turned on his heel and walked from the circle of elders.

"What is the brother of my dead husband to do now?" snarled the bitter woman, Fox Tail. She had been in mourning for less than a week since the loss of her man in the fight with the Ute and their white man friend, each day seemingly making her more and more bitter and angry. "The elders of the council are weak! The women of the village could do more! Those old men just sit around and talk while the young warriors try to provide for the village and bring honor to the people. Their weakness is like they spit on the memory of our men!" She glanced to Bear Chaser, the wife of Many Bears as she sat silently working on the beadwork on her man's moccasins. "Do you have nothing to say? It is your man who should get vengeance to honor his brother and my man!"

Bear Chaser glanced up at the bitter woman, shook her head slightly and answered softly, "My man is a great warrior! He led others to go for the Ute but the Arapaho, our enemies, interfered!" She looked up as Many Bears strode into their circle, and recognized he was angry, and when he was angry, she had learned to keep her silence.

Following close behind Many Bears, Crazy Hawk and Rattling Voice, followed their friend into his lodge where Many Bears dropped down to be seated before the smoldering coals of the lodge fire. Bears waved toward the nearby blankets for Hawk and Voice to be seated. He growled as he looked at the two men, "I have decided to leave this village of cowards and old men! Will you join me?"

Hawk and Voice looked at one another, surprise showing on their faces, "What did the council say?" asked Crazy Hawk.

"The old man said we had failed and brought death and shame on the village! They turned their backs on me after saying I could no longer lead! LEAD!? I can lead! They are the ones who failed! They failed to avenge the deaths of my brother and the others who were killed by the Ute! It is their failure that brought death and shame, not us!" snarled Many Bears.

"Now you will leave the village, but where will you go?" asked Rattling Voice.

"Go? Anywhere! The valley with the buffalo where the Ute hunted has much game and water! Or perhaps we will take our vengeance on the white man and take their valley for our own!" He glowered at the two men, stood and beat his chest, "We are the *Pibianigwai* people of the *Yaparuhka* band of the people. We do not ask where we are to go, we go where we want!" He turned away, ducked out of the entryway of the hide lodge, looked at Bear Chaser, "Woman! We are hungry!" as he motioned to his friends that came from the lodge.

Bear Chaser and Fox Tail hurriedly served the three men with the stew and fry bread, listening as they served. It was not the place of a woman to speak when the men are speaking, nor to insert themselves in any of the conversations, and the women did their best to hang back and tend to the needs of the men as they argued among themselves. When Many Bears sent the two away to recruit more warriors, Bear Chaser asked, "Do you mean we are to leave the village?"

"What is it to you? You do as you are told!" growled Many Bears, glancing to Fox Tail and back to Bear Chaser.

"This woman will not leave unless you bring me the scalp of the man who killed your brother!" hissed Fox Tail as she gathered the carved trenchers used to serve the men the stew. She glared at Bear Chaser, "How could you go with a man that cannot even avenge his own brother? What kind of warrior is he?" nodding toward Many Bears. The man jumped to his feet and grabbed a piece of nearby firewood and raised it to strike Fox Tail, but she snatched a long-bladed knife from her belt and held it sharp edge up as she dropped into a crouch. Her lip curled in a snarl, her eyes squinted, and she held the knife ready to strike. Many Bears knew if he missed, she could easily strike with the knife.

"Do it! Try to hit me! I will split you from your crotch to your throat and rip your innards out and throw them on the fire before you take another step!" threatened Fox Tail.

Many Bears paused in his movement, remembering that this woman could have become a warrior, but chose to unite with his brother. She had proven herself a capable fighter and hunter as was required of a warrior, and she had a reputation with her knife. He looked at the woman, saw reckless determination and a lust for blood in her eyes. He took a deep breath, stepped back, and dropped the stick, mumbling.

He glanced up as Crazy Hawk walked back into the light of the fire. He looked from Many Bears to Fox Tail, frowned, and motioned to Many Bears to walk with him. The two men left the ring of light, but their words were heard by the women. "Some have said they would come to fight, but to leave the village . . ." started Crazy Hawk, then paused, "*but* if we were to go for vengeance as we started before and came back to the village with scalps and more, it would prove you are a great warrior and leader, and many would come with us to make a new village with you as our leader!"

Many Bears stopped, turning to look at his friend, "How many will go with us?"

Crazy Hawk thought a moment, considering, "Walks Alone, Rattling Voice, me, and perhaps one hand of others. But if we return with a victory, many more!"

"Then go! Tell the others we leave at first light!"

15 / SNARES

From the campsite, the creek in the rift split the foot-hills that sided the river near the mouth of the long canyon that took the Arkansa river south. At the dog-leg in the trail beside the creek, with the aspen thicket covering both sides, Gabe and Cougar set their first snare. Cougar grinned as she envisioned what they should do, and quickly took charge. "Cut a tall sapling, about the size of your wrist and twice as tall as you! But get it from far back so the fresh cut won't show!" she ordered as she slipped from the appaloosa, ground tying her to begin her set-up. The aspen near the trail were close-in and tall, straight, and about the size of a man's thigh, suitable for what Cougar planned. She picked a tight group of four close trees, bare trunks up to about ten or twelve feet, and stripped out a length of rope for her purpose.

As she finagled and worked on the set-up, she

glanced up the steep slope and noticed a slight overhang with loose shale and sizeable boulders on top.
She grinned again and as soon as Gabe returned
with the aspen sapling, she stepped back and pointed at the overhang, "It would be easy to make that
into a slide," she suggested, looking at Gabe with a
wicked grin. He laughed and started up the steep
hillside to set the trap.

The confluence of the creek and river forced the trail
to the far side of the river, the crossing marked by
a mid-stream gravel bar. Once on the east side, the
trail lay in the shadow of tall granite cliffs that rose
two to three hundred feet above the river. The grey
and brown streaked stone looming like an ancient
ogre as it shadowed the narrow trail. "Now that's a
great spot for a rockslide!" offered Gabe, looking to
the crest of the cliffs where a pair of scraggly piñon
held a tenuous grip in a jagged crack of the granite. "Don't think it'd take much to set one up, but
the trick is getting it to slide. Any ideas?" he asked,
looking to Cougar who was looking high above as
she shaded her eyes.

Cougar frowned, dropped her eyes to look around
near the trail. They were less than a half-mile upstream from the confluence of the creek and the river,
as Cougar suggested, "Let's go back there," nodding
to the south end of the cliffs, "I think there is a trail

that will take us to the top."

The time-worn trail was little more than a sel-dom-used game trail that allowed the deer and bighorns to come to water, but it allowed Gabe and Cougar access to the back side of the cliffs. Cougar led the way through the winding gulley and rounded a point with a big rock outcropping and suddenly reined up, frowning as she looked at the rocks. She held her hand up to stop Gabe, bent slightly to the side and listened. She turned to look at Gabe, "Something else we might use," and stepped down, ground tying the appy. She picked up a long fork ended stick that lay at the edge of some aspen, stripped off the loose bark and started up the draw beside the rocks. Gabe had stepped down, but watched her, unknowing of what she was doing or planning. Within moments, she was back, smiling. "Get the parfleche off the pack horse, we will need it."

"Uh, what for?" asked Gabe as he stepped beside the big grey packhorse and fidgeted with the parfleche.

"You'll see," answered a grinning Cougar.

"That's what I'm afraid of," grumbled Gabe. He had the parfleche in hand and followed Cougar as she returned to the rocks. Within a few steps, he stopped, frozen in place, eyes wide, as he heard what had inter-ested Cougar. The buzzing of many rattles told him she had found a nest of rattlesnakes! He looked at her as she grinned at him, "How you gonna do this?"

"Just sit it down, open it up, and step back."

"How far back?" asked Gabe, hopefully.

Cougar laughed, turned away and moved closer to the nest. She stretched out with the long stick, finagled around a little, then stepped back with a snake coiled around the stick. She deftly dropped it into the parfleche, flipped the lid shut, and turned around. She looked at Gabe, grinning, "You will need to open it when I get another one!" laughing. "But you can get a stick to do it, if you want."

Gabe looked around, spotted a long stick, and ran to pick it up, quickly returning to his place well back from the parfleche. Cougar grinned, shaking her head, and returned to her task. Within a short while, she had retrieved four good sized snakes and dropped them into the now closed parfleche. She said, "I think they're getting crowded, so that will be plenty."

"That's more than enough as far as I'm concerned. The last time I handled snakes was when me'n Ezra went against them Paiutes, and that was enough snake handling for a lifetime!"

"Then put it back on the pack, and we will go to the top of the cliffs to see what we will do next!" she declared, still smiling broadly, and enjoying her husband's vexing.

Once atop the bluff with the cliffs below, Gabe decided to use his scope and have another look-see.

They were high enough he could see over the low hills on the other side of the river and into the wide-open valley beyond. If the Comanche were coming, he could easily see them. He slowly scanned the rift and bluff where they had camped, the long bluff that fronted the mesa that stretched across the flat of the valley. If the Comanche came from the south, they would have to cross that mesa and drop off the long bluff, probably one of the two cuts where the mesa was split by run-off creeks. He searched for any movement, dust, or fleeing animals that would show the approach of riders, but there was nothing. With a quick survey of the far ridges at the base of the foothills below the mountains, a look at the valley below the white cliffs, and a close-in look at the nearby hills, he saw nothing but some small game and a few deer. He shook his head and lifted the scope for another scan of the long mesa and saw nothing, until something caught his eye just as he was lowering the scope. Wolf came to his feet beside him, staring into the distance, and Gabe brought his scope back to focus on the edge of the rift. A wispy cloud of dust rose, and he focused the scope again, twisting the barrel, and searched. Then he saw them, about a half-dozen riders, maybe more, coming at a steady gait, but not in a hurry. He sucked in a deep breath, shook his head as he rolled to the side and pushed the scope closed.

"They're comin', looks like six or seven that I could tell. They're on the mesa above that bluff where we camped, so they'll be a while gettin' here."

Cougar stood beside her appy, nodded, and said, "While you looked, I looked." She pointed back along the trail below, "That last knob there beside the trail, this side of the crossing."

Gabe looked where she pointed, as she continued, "If I take the snakes, from on top I could throw them down on the riders below. Their horses will stampede this way, you can drop the rockslide on them. I can leave from that draw below the knob. You can circle around here," pointing behind them, "take that draw and cross the river there," pointing to a place upstream of the cliffs. "We can meet beyond those hills," pointing to the hills on the far side of the river that edged the big valley, "and decide what to do next."

"Yeah, that'll prob'ly work. So, guess I better get busy stackin' rocks!"

"Unless you would rather throw snakes!" giggled Cougar, enjoying Gabe's discomfort.

With a quick embrace, they separated, Wolf staying with Gabe as each turned to their tasks. Gabe located a log of a downed juniper, stripped off the dead branches and took it near the edge of the cliff. With two fist sized rocks, each wrapped with rope, he set the log in place on the edge of the cliff and on the low side of the top slope. But all the while he worked, he was troubled, something just did not feel right about what they were doing, but it had to be done. They were here to protect their family at the cabin, it was better to take the fight to the enemy than to sit back and wait. He stacked rocks behind and on top of the log, carefully placing each one so the stack was dependent on the ones underneath that pushed against the log. He stripped off his shirt, sweat dripping off his chest, neck, forehead, and arms, and worked as quickly as his strength allowed. He soon had a stack of rocks as high as he could reach, and the weight pushed against the log and the smaller rocks that stabilized the pile. He looked over his handiwork, and satisfied, sat down to wipe off the sweat and replace his buckskin shirt. The stack was between a couple of scraggly piñons and not readily visible from below, but Gabe's view of the valley and the canyon below was unhindered. Now he would wait.

Cougar was in place just a short while after leaving Gabe atop the cliffs. The trail behind the cliffs was joined by a trail that cut behind a timber covered hill and met another game trail that bottomed a dry gulch leading to the river. She cut behind a thicket of juniper, dropped behind the lone knob that would be her launching point and tethered her appaloosa and the grey pack horse in the draw behind. With parfleche in hand, she climbed the back side of the rocky knob, crested out on top and found a rocky flat on the precipice and seated herself behind a low growing juniper to wait for the Comanche. From her promontory, she could see straight up the creek where the first trap had been set. She smiled as she envisioned what would happen when they rode into those aspen and her snare. She chuckled to herself and settled down to wait.

16 / CAUTION

Many Bears led the small war party from the village just as the eastern sky was showing a wide band of pale blue. Heavy dark clouds were layered above, and the bottoms lightly tinted with pink and the men rode from the quiet village. Many Bears was sided by Crazy Hawk and once free from the village, Hawk suggested, "Rattling Voice knows where the camp of the Ute and the lodge of the white man are, perhaps he should scout ahead."

Many Bears nodded, "Yes, but not until we are into the valley of the buffalo. We are few and the village of the Ute is large, we cannot lose even one of our men."

"A warrior that is worried about losing or dying will not be the warrior he must be, he will be a danger to those with him!" declared Crazy Hawk. "Every man must be willing to give his life for his people, it is a great honor!"

"Those that died under the hooves of the buffalo, died because they became afraid and did not listen, but they died and when they crossed over it was without honor!" stated Many Bears, remembering the futile attack against the Arapaho and the buffalo stampede.

Crazy Hawk fell silent, glancing to Many Bears as they rode together. They came from the canyon of the Arkansa and stopped. Many Bears motioned for Crazy Hawk to cross the river and take to the hill on the far side to scout the land before them. As Crazy Hawk's mount splashed across the river, Many Bears knew he was showing an uncustomary caution by sending a scout as he did, but the chastisement from the leaders had burned and he was determined they would return to the village, victorious and with scalps and plunder to prove the elders wrong. If caution was necessary, then so be it.

Many Bears waved Rattling Voice to come beside him, watched as the man nudged his horse forward and asked, "The Ute village and the lodge of the white man, how far?"

Rattling Voice stood in his stirrups and shaded his eyes to look in the distance, he pointed to the north and the many peaks of the Sawatch range, "The third mountain. At the bottom there are white cliffs. The village is there, the white man's lodge on this side of the valley, below the long ridge."

"When you went with the others to take the horses,

which way?"

"You were with the hunting party that watched the Ute and the buffalo?" asked Rattling Voice.

"Yes."

"We followed the river from there, then the creek that comes from the canyon of the white cliffs. When we came near, we were led into the trees behind the white man's lodge where the horses were kept in a big meadow," explained Rattling Voice, looking toward the valley to avoid looking directly at Many Bears. He had grown afraid of the man, even though they had been friends since their youth, Bears had grown intolerant of others and surly in his attitude.

Crazy Hawk came from the river, "There is nothing in the valley as far as I can see. Even the buffalo have moved toward the mountains."

"Good. We will stay on this trail," nodding to the path before them, "stay on this side of the river until it comes from the canyon. We will go the same way Black Bear led us as a hunting party before the Ute took the buffalo."

Crazy Hawk swung his mount around and took to the trail beside Many Bears as they led off from the canyon, pointing toward the east edge of the wide valley. The men and horses were painted for war, their minds full of images of battle and blood, but the clouds had dissipated and now showed a clear blue sky, warm sun, and birds singing contrasted with those thoughts and images and brought the eyes and minds to other things. It was strange to see smiles split the faces of war painted warriors, but it was one of those days when everything was right. Flowers splashed the side of the trail with brilliant blues, purples, yellows and white. Rabbits scurried under cover of sage and rabbit brush but stopped to look back at the intruders to their land. A big buck, velvet antlers crowning his majestic head, took the hillside in bounds, but stopped and turned to look at the passersby.

It was approaching late morning when they took the trail that dropped from the rim of the gorge that came from the deeper canyon, and crossed the river, to mount the opposite side and follow the trail that shadowed the tree line of the foothills. By mid-day, they crested the bluff of the long mesa and took the easier trail at the edge of the tree line. When they bottomed out in the rift with the creek, Many Bears motioned for the men to stop. "We will rest the horses, take some food, then move into the draw there," pointing to the narrow draw that carried the creek to the confluence with the Arkansa river.

Gabe retrieved his scope from the saddle bags and returned to his promontory beside the rocks. He stretched out the scope, searched for the Comanche and spotted the horses just below the long bluff near where he and Cougar had camped. He could see them clearly now, counted the horses and tallied nine. He shook his head, knowing those were not the best odds, nine against two, but if it was to be, he would rather face them now than later. But his gut churned, and he shook his head at the thought. He and Cougar were lying in wait to ambush this band they were certain was bound for their lodge to attack their family and steal their goods, but what if they were just on a hunt? Yet the war paint said otherwise. Or what if they were bound elsewhere and had nothing in mind for him and the family? He argued with himself as he watched the men lounge in the shade letting their horses graze and take water. He took a deep breath and knew what he must do, it was not in him just to attack men and seek to kill without knowing for certain his own life or the lives of his loved ones were in danger.

He rose from his perch, replaced the scope in the saddle bags, tightened the girth on Ebony and swung aboard, motioning Wolf to take to the trail off the bluff. The trail dropped between the buttes and Gabe took to the river, Wolf swimming alongside, to cross to a shoulder he spotted from the top of the cliffs. He tethered Ebony, slipped the case with the Mongol bow from under the left stirrup leather, and sat down to string the deadly weapon. He hung the quiver from his belt and started to the shoulder with the scattered juniper to climb up to the rocky outcropping. He settled down bedside the big rock that sat tenuously on the shoulder above the creek, shielded by the juniper, and scanned the narrow arroyo with the aspen and the first of their snares. From his perch, he could see the upper end of the arroyo and saw movement as the Comanche were mounting and preparing to start on the trail that would lead to the confluence.

Cougar Woman saw her man come from the narrow draw and take to the water, Wolf alongside, and watched him tether the big black and start up the shoulder of the towering bluff. She shook her head, knowing he was up to something and trusting whatever it was, was for the best. She took a deep breath and settled in to watch.

Gabe nocked one of the whistler arrows, picked his target and leaned back to prepare to send the arrow on its course. The average bowman with the typical bow of the plains tribes, could send an arrow with considerable accuracy as far as a hundred yards, usually much less. Beyond that was difficult at best and impossible for most. However, the Mongol bow with its laminated limbs and recurve construction and in the hands of a master with the weapon, could easily launch an arrow with accuracy as far as four hundred yards, an unbelievable distance for most to understand. Because of the elevation of his promontory and the slight slope of the valley with the creek, Gabe chose a spot in the middle of the draw where the trail was exposed, and the trees set back. With the jade thumb ring and the typical wrap grip for a shooter of a Mongol bow, he brought the bow to full draw, lifted the tip of the arrow, and let the shaft whisper away. Within just a few feet, the arrow began its shrill whistle that sounded more like a scream, and it arched high overhead, crested the arch, and started to plummet to earth, the scream echoing between the walls of the arroyo.

At the strange sound overhead, Many Bears reined up, frowning as he lifted his eyes to the sky, expecting to see a circling eagle or some other bird of prey, but he had never heard a scream such as this, and it grew louder and louder, so much so that the horses grew skittish and searched for the source of the scream. As they fought to control their mounts, the Comanches' eyes grew large as they searched the sky for the scream. As the arrow plummeted to the earth, Many Bears horse started to rear up, but his rider pulled the rein taut, jerking the mount's chin down to his chest. The blue roan gelding back stepped, nervously searching for footing, fighting the bit, and the arrow drove into the ground less than three feet before the horse, eliciting a screaming whinny from the animal.

"Aiieee! What is this?!" shouted Many Bears, seeing the black arrow with the long shaft quiver in the ground, shaking from the impact, fletching fluttering in the air. Many Bears jumped to the ground, searching the hillsides for the shooter, but saw nothing. The warriors also searched, shouting to one another, pointing to the hillsides expecting to see a hail of arrows from on high, but nothing came. As the horses were brought under control and the men drew silent, Many Bears stood beside his horse, still searching for the shooter, expecting more arrows to come, and silence fell.

The birds had quieted, the distant water in the canyon gave a muffled roar as the raging waters entered the high-walled canyon, the quakies fluttered their silver bottomed leaves, the nervous horses pranced, but the arroyo was quiet. Then a voice came from below, "Many Bears! You bring your men to their death!" the words were in the tongue of the Shoshone, but the dialects of the Algonquian tribes were similar and understood by the Comanche.

"Who dares to speak such things to the Comanche!" barked Many Bears, his words echoing through the arroyo.

"I am Spirit Bear! White Knife told your people of me! I grant you mercy if you leave, but if you come further, you and your men will die!"

Many Bears motioned to Crazy Hawk and Walks Alone, sending them to either side of the draw to search for the shooter. He watched as they took to the hillsides, then turned back to the lower end, "You are but one man! We have many! We are not afraid! You killed my brother, and your scalp will hang from my coup stick before this day is over!"

"If your brother was with White Knife, he died bravely trying to steal my horses. But you bring more men to die, this should not be. You will cause the women of your village to mourn for many days!"

Many Bears watched Crazy Hawk and Walks Alone as they moved through the sparse trees, searching for the shooter, but they turned back to look at Many Bears, shrugged to show there was no sign within range of a shooter. Many Bears motioned them back and spoke again, "You have sent one arrow and run away, why should we fear a coward?"

Many Bears had no sooner uttered the words when another arrow whispered through the air and buried itself less than two feet from the first arrow. Many Bears jumped back, looking quickly to Crazy Hawk and Walks Alone, but they had seen nothing. Many Bears swung back aboard his horse, waved Rattling Voice into the lead to scout the trail, nudging his horse to follow as the two scouts rejoined the band.

17 / CLASH

Gabe slid and stumbled down the steep slope below the talus, returning to Ebony. Quickly returning the bow to the case and hanging the quiver beside the cantle of the saddle, he swung aboard and dug his heels into Ebony's ribs to quickly cross the river and take to the trail between the buttes to return to his promontory above the cliffs. As he came from the river, he looked up to the top of the nearby butte, waved to Cougar Woman but did not see any sign of his woman, yet was confident she was still lying-in wait for the Comanche.

As Gabe hurried to the cliff top, the Comanche started down the trail and were entering the thicket of aspen. Cougar Woman had intentionally set the trip for the snare at the side of the trail, knowing the manner of most warriors to not follow directly behind one another, often taking to the edge of the trail to see past the one before them. Rattling Voice was in the lead, cautiously searching the trail and hillsides for any enemy, yet moving quickly to scout well ahead of the others. Many Bears followed, with Crazy Hawk close behind keeping to the right side of the trail, followed by Walks Alone who held to the left edge of the trail. The scout, the leader, and Crazy Hawk passed the camouflaged trip rope, but the horse of Walks Alone stepped on the rope and the peg holding it taut. The aspen sapling that was bent well back, whipped around, carrying the deadly sharpened sticks in a sweeping arch, and caught Walks Alone in the face, neck, and chest. He screamed as he tumbled backwards off his horse, spooking the horses behind him, and the trigger of the rockslide was tethered to the sapling, releasing the deadfall and rocks from high above. In an instant, the rockslide began its steep descent, taking everything in its path, flattening the piñon, juniper, and aspen saplings, to crash down on the trail, driving the last two of the war party to stumble and fall into the creek below the trail, fighting to escape the thundering rockslide.

The sharpened sticks that had been tied into the branches of the aspen sapling drove into the face and neck of Walks Alone, one piercing his eye, another ripping at his cheek, another burying itself in his throat. The death it dealt was painful and bloody, but if he was still alive after the impalement, the rocks had taken what was left of his spirit and buried his body under tons of debris. The two riders that had been knocked from the trail were battered and bruised, but still alive as they struggled from the brush, rocks, and water in the creek bottom. One of the horses had tumbled under the rocks and only one leg showed under the pile of rocks, the other stood nervously on the slope above the brush, trembling and looking around, searching for a way back to the trail.

Many Bears, Crazy Hawk, and Rattling Voice had stopped and stepped down, looking behind them at the rising dust and the massive rock pile. Many Bears looked at the hillside above, saw no evidence of anyone or anything that could have caused the slide, shook his head, and looked at Crazy Hawk. "How did that happen?"

Hawk looked at the leader, shaking his head, "The man who shot the arrows! He did it! He warned you we would die!"

"But we have no choice! We cannot return that way!" he declared motioning to the blocked trail with the rockslide. "Go, get the others!" he ordered, motioning to both Crazy Hawk and Rattling Voice. As the two men walked back to survey the damage, Many Bears turned to look down the narrow draw that carried the small creek to the confluence, searching for any sign of other snares or ambushes. There was nothing to indicate anyone waited. With the silence that returned after the rockslide, he heard other birds, looked high to see a circling Osprey, saw nothing that would be a giveaway of any danger. He shook his head, and breathed deep, waiting for the others to return.

The horse that had carried Walks Alone stood in the trail, reins dragging, but the body of Walks Alone was buried in the rubble. Crazy Hawk returned, with one man walking, the others riding, some coming from below the trail, others closer. He looked at Crazy Hawk, "One man is dead, another lost his horse, two were injured, but they live to fight."

"Have him take the horse there," pointing to the standing mount that had been Walks Alone's. "We go!" declared Many Bears as he swung aboard his mount. He led the way, Crazy Hawk trailing close behind as they entered the water to cross the shallow waters of the river at the crossing with the long gravel bar. As they came from the water, Many Bears turned north on the narrow trail that hugged the tall butte and started toward the upper end of the long canyon. Every man was watchful, but the narrow trail was so close to the steep-sided bluff, the only possible point of attack would be further on where the trail widened. They looked across the river, searching for any give away of an attack, saw nothing and visibly relaxed.

Cougar Woman saw the band cross the river, watched as they took to the trail. She lifted the parfleche, shook it to stir up the rattle snakes, then lifted it high overhead, stepped close to the edge to look down. She wanted to time the drop so the snakes would hit the last riders, forcing the leaders to charge into the upper reaches toward the cliffs. With another glance below, she tilted the parfleche, letting the weight of the big snakes open the flaps and watched as the serpents fell. Withing seconds, the screams and whinnying came from below as the snakes landed on the riders and the horses.

Cougar Woman quickly secured the empty parfleche to the packs on the big grey, tightened the girth on her appaloosa, swung aboard and took off at a run to take the trail that shadowed the hills that lined the east shore of the river. Once she cleared the line of hills, the trail cut toward the river giving her access to a crossing and the trail that cut through the rolling hills on the west side. The previously chosen route, round about though it was, was less than five miles to the rendezvous point and she pulled up atop the long ridge that lay beyond the rift with the creek on the north side, and the river on the east.

When the snakes fell from the sky, one landed on the last warrior, wrapping itself around his neck and burying its fangs in the man's neck, time and again, as the man fought both the snake and the bucking horse, but he soon lost his fight with both and tumbled from his horse, falling down the side of the trail and splashing into the white-water rapids of the river. The other snakes landed on the horses of other riders, one landing on the ground before the next to the last horse, causing the mount to rear up and start bucking. The rider grabbed at his tall pommel, the other hand grabbing a handful of mane, as the panicked horse went airborne! The mount bent in half and kicked back at the blue sky, burying its face between his front feet, stretching out as if the longer he stretched, the better his chances of escape from the snakes. But the mount reared up again, pawed at the clouds, then sun fished, showing its belly to the mid-day sun as it twisted in the air, its rider flying free to land in a heap on the trail, only to be trampled by the horse of the snake bit rider.

The other horses had stampeded, several bucking and stomping, anything to escape the attack of flying snakes. They stormed from the narrow trail beside the tall butte, only to break into the open, allowing ample space for the horses to do everything to rid themselves of their riders. The only mount that was under control was the blue roan ridden by Many Bears, but the others were soon brought to a stop, the riders, reaching down to stroke the animals' necks and comfort the panicked horses. Crazy Hawk glared at Many Bears, "We were told this man was a great warrior! We have lost three warriors and we have not even seen this man or his woman!"

"What is there to do?! We cannot go back! We must stay on this trail and we will get our vengeance! Would you have one man drive us away?!" snarled Many Bears, looking from Crazy Hawk to the others. He glared at Rattling Voice, Crazy Hawk and the three young warriors who showed only fear. They had not been proven in battle and had come to gain honors and earn their place as warriors, but they had to live to gain that privilege. They nervously looked around, searching the hillsides, riverbanks, and the trail, but nothing told of any danger.

"Come! We will leave this place!" declared Many Bears as he jerked the head of the blue roan around to once again take the trail. He looked before him to see the narrow trail that seemed to hang on the side of the steep sheer cliff face. The towering granite stretching over two hundred feet high. He twisted around in his saddle, "There is no place for an attack there! We are safe!" declared Many Bears, growling the words to the others. He turned back to look at the trail and nudged his mount forward.

As Many Bears led the four men, the clatter of the hooves echoed back from the opposite side of the narrow gorge, the echo seemingly louder than the rattle of the hooves, making it sound as if there were dozens of riders. High above, Gabe fought with the rope holding the small rocks beneath the log. He jerked, pulled, struggled to make them move. He was ready to drop the rope and try to wiggle them with his hands and move at least one of the rocks, when he saw the bigger rocks move. He jerked again, causing some small rocks and dirt slip over the edge, then the two trigger stones gave way to his pull, they jerked loose, and the log started to slip, then roll as the heavier rocks began to fall. Then the entire pile gave way and plummeted over the edge.

When the tumbling of a few small stones bounced on the trail before him, Many Bears leaned to the side to look high above, only to see the big stones plunging down towards them. He slapped legs to his mount as he screamed to the men, "Run! Now!" as his horse lunged forward, digging his heels into the rocky trail. The big horse made three long jumps as the first rocks crashed to the bottom, some bouncing off the walls of the cliffs, others splashing into the river. A quick glance back showed riders, ducking, hands over heads, as their horses ran, stumbling, trying to escape. Rocks rattled and thundered, dust rose, horses screamed, warriors shouted, and the roar of the rockslide echoed across the narrow gorge.

The thunder of the rockfall resounded down the valley, smothering all other sound, the dust filled the canyon and slowly settled over the water to be carried away as if it were never there. As the roar subsided, Many Bears sat his mount, Crazy Hawk beside him on one side, Rattling Voice on the other, as they looked long faced at the pile of rocks, knowing the three other warriors were buried in the rubble. No one spoke as Many Bears stepped down and went to stand beside the rubble. Slowly, quietly, the other warriors joined him. Unknown and unseen, a lone rider with a wolf beside him crossed the river about five hundred yards behind and upstream from them.

18 / CONFRONTATION

"There's three left, an' I'm purty sure one of 'ems the leader called Many Bears! He's a stubborn one!" declared Gabe as he reined up beside Cougar Woman.

"You gave them warning!" responded an angry Cougar Woman, angry because of the Comanche that dared to come against her and her man and to threaten their family.

"Yeah, but as it happens, the leader's the one that makes the decisions and it's the others that have to shed their blood and lose their lives because of the leader's stupidity and stubbornness." Gabe shook his head and spat a mouthful of dust to the side. He had crossed the river and ridden around the rocky point to meet up with Cougar. Behind her, he saw standing tall across the valley, the peaks of the Sawatch range scratched at the clear blue of the early summer sky, the remains of winter's snow hiding in the deeper crevasses and coloring the grey/blue peaks with streaks of white that shone bright in the early afternoon sun. The black shoulders of the massive mountains faded into the shades of green and tan of the valley bottom, and just over Cougar's shoulder, the white cliffs supported the black shoulders of the taller peaks and marked the place where their family waited expectantly.

"If they cross where you did, they will see your sign and follow," observed Cougar, pointing with her chin at the tracks of Ebony that led from the river.

Gabe twisted in his saddle to look back toward the river, noted his tracks and nodded, "But they could decide to stay near the river to try to come up the arroyo yonder to attack our cabin."

"Not if they choose to return to their village," suggested Cougar, hopefully and nodded toward the trail.

Gabe quickly looked back to see the three Comanche start to cross the river. He turned back, motioned to Cougar, "Up there!" nodding to the point of rocks above the trail that circumvented the knob beside them.

Cougar slipped from the appy, dropped the reins to ground tie her and the grey pack horse as Gabe swung Ebony around to wait for the warriors. A notch in the rocks offered him a view of the river bank and flat land between him and the river. He would wait until their movements revealed their choice to either return to the village or continue on their vengeance quest.

Once on the flats, the three reined up and one pointed to the mountains, speaking to the others. The leader showed his anger as he motioned and hollered at the others, shaking his head as he pointed to the south end of the valley, probably toward their village. He muttered something more, defiantly staring at the others as he jerked at the reins of his mount to turn to face the others as if daring them to respond.

Gabe nudged Ebony from the rocks, moved into the open along the trail toward the river. He started to approach the Comanche, unseen, until one of the men shouted and pointed. The others turned to look, the leader shouting as he grabbed for his weapons.

"You do that, you'll die!" shouted Gabe and he kicked Ebony to a trot to come close to the warriors. He held his right hand high, palm open and facing the warriors, then lifted his other hand that held only the reins. "There is an arrow pointed at your chest!" he nodded to the top of the rocks, "If you want to die, grab your bow or lance!"

The three men looked at each other, the leader frowning as he shaded his eyes to see Cougar Woman slowly stand, arrow nocked and bow at full draw, standing above them on the rocks. Gabe said, "I gave you a warning. Your men did not have to die. You do not have to die. If you choose to return to your village and never come back painted for war, you are free to leave. We will not stop you."

Many Bears glanced to Rattling Voice, his expression asking a question that the man answered with a nod. Many Bears turned back to face Gabe, "You are the one who killed our brothers! I would have your scalp on my lance!" he spat, his lip curling in a snarl of contempt.

"If you speak of those that were killed when they raided my horse herd, yes, I am the one who killed them. As you would do if someone came into your village to steal your horses. Is this the one that ran away instead of staying to fight with White Knife and your brothers?" asked Gabe, pointing to Rattling Voice with his chin.

Rattling Voice shouted, "I did not run away! I killed three Ute before I left to tell my people about the battle!"

Gabe shook his head, laughed a little, then looked at Many Bears with a stern expression, "You ride with a coward that runs away when there is a fight or when your warriors need a man at their side! He did not kill any Ute warriors, there were no Ute there! Just me and my woman," nodding toward the rocks above them. "And you! You lead your men to death after they have been warned! You led your men against my friends, the Arapaho, and your men died. Will you have these die also?" he asked as he pointed to Crazy

Hawk and Rattling Voice.

Gabe looked directly at Crazy Hawk, "If you would live, you are free to go and take that," nodding to Rattling Voice, "with you. We will not stop you. But if you choose to stay with Many Bears, I will kill you after I kill him!"

Many Bears was angered and grabbed for his tomahawk, but before he could bring it from his belt, he was staring at the barrels of Gabe's over/under saddle pistol. The cocking of the hammer made Many Bears eyes widen as he froze in his movement, looking at Gabe. Without looking at the others, Gabe asked, "Well? Are you leaving or staying?"

Crazy Hawk looked at Rattling Voice who was obviously frightened as he was nervously fidgeting in his seat, looking from the warrior on the rocks to the man with the pistol pointed at Many Bears. Crazy Hawk answered, "I cannot leave. He is the leader of our party and he is my friend."

"What about you?" asked Gabe, nodding toward Rattling Voice. "You ran away before, you running again?"

Rattling Voice looked from the white man to Many Bears and Crazy Hawk, knowing that if he ran and they lived, he would be banished from the people and probably die alone. He shook his head, dropped his eyes, "I cannot leave."

"Well, well. Now what do we do? How 'bout you

Many Bears? You ready to leave?"

"We are the *Pibianigwai* warriors of the *Yaparuhka* band of the *Numunuu*, Comanche! We do not run! We will fight!" spat Many Bears.

"I was afraid you'd say that. Alright then." He looked up at Cougar Woman, "Come on down, Cougar. This fella wants to fight!" He waited, resting his elbow on his saddle horn, the pistol still pointed at Many Bears, as Cougar came from the rocks. When she stepped beside him, he looked down at her, "You make sure those two mind their manners," nodding toward Crazy Hawk and Rattling Voice. "Me'n Many Bears there are gonna finish this here'n now."

As Cougar watched the others, Gabe holstered the pistol and swung his leg over Ebony's rump and stepped to the ground. He looked at Many Bears, "Alright Many Bears, c'mon down and let's get this done with. You can have your knife and hawk, and just you'n me'll go at it. Your friends there can watch or leave, their choice, but if they try anything, my woman or Wolf there," nodding toward the big black wolf that stood at the ready beside Ebony, "will kill them!"

Gabe motioned for Crazy Hawk and Rattling Voice to get down and tether their horses and Many Bears' blue roan.

Gabe stuck his belt pistol in the pommel of his saddle, twisted at the waist to flex his muscles, and smiled and nodded at Cougar Woman who smiled in return, showing her unconcern about the pending fight. She knew her man and knew what he could do, and also knew that Many Bears was the typical warrior who aspired to be a leader but had never proven himself to be anything other than a common warrior and a typical fighter. She also knew he was in for a surprise when he went against her man.

Wolf stood beside Cougar as they watched Gabe stand before Many Bears. Beyond the two combatants, Crazy Hawk and Rattling Voice stood, feet widespread, looking at their leader and the white man about to fight one another. Crazy Hawk spoke softly to Rattling Voice, "If Many Bears falls, we must kill the white man and his woman before Bears can be killed." Rattling Voice glanced at his friend, nodded slightly, and looked back to the space between them and the woman and the wolf. He asked, "The wolf?"

"After we kill the man and his woman, then we kill the wolf."

19 / FIGHT

Gabe had his tomahawk in his belt, his knives hung from the harness between his shoulders at his back, but he stood before Many Bears empty handed. The Comanche had his hawk in his left hand, the knife in his right. He dropped into a crouch, hands extended from his sides, glaring at Gabe and started to circle, moving to his right. Gabe stood erect, slowly dropped into a slight crouch, pivoting to watch Bears as he moved. The Comanche was confident he could easily and quickly finish this as he lunged forward; his knife extended. His move with the knife right of center, was to make Gabe step toward the hand with the hawk, giving Bears a quick strike to finish. But Gabe did just the opposite, pivoted further to the left, making the lunge of Bears and the extended knife pass close to his middle. Gabe grinned and stepped back, making no move against Bears, but chuckled as he stepped clear.

Bears scowled, screamed his war cry with a high pitched, "Aaiiiiieeee!" as he made a quick step toward Gabe and swung his knife in a wide arch expected to slit Gabe's middle, but the knife whiffed through the air, connecting with nothing. Gabe pivoted again, grabbing Bears arm with both hands as Bears completed the arc, off balance with the miss. Gabe jerked Bears arm high, bringing it straight down and driving his elbow to the ground, pushing his wrist down and pinning it with his left hand, driving his knee into Bears solar plexus and knocking Bears wind out, then twisting the pinned wrist and freeing the knife. Gabe stepped back, jerking Bears to his feet, but without his knife. Gabe quickly kicked the knife away, watching as Bears stepped back and moved his tomahawk to his right hand.

Gabe grinned again, shaking his head, watching Bears eyes to anticipate his moves. Suddenly the man cocked his arm back to throw the hawk, but Gabe slipped his hawk from his belt and as the weapon of Bears tumbled end over end toward him, Gabe knocked it aside, then casually tossed his own hawk aside with another grin and shaking his head. "Now what Many Bears? You have no weapons?" with a shrug, continuing to move to the side as they circled one another. Bears lunged forward, arms outstretched, but Gabe leaned in, grabbed Bears by the long braids, pulled his head forward and lowered his own to smash the Comanche's face against his skull, eliciting a scream from the man, as he heard the man's nose crunch and teeth break.

Gabe released him and stepped back, grinning and shaking his head, as he looked at the blood splattered face and flattened nose of Many Bears. Blood came from his nose and mouth, hatred spilled from his eyes, as he wiped his forearm across his face. He spat two teeth to the ground, glared at Gabe and lowered his head and shoulders and charged. Gabe made a half step to the side, twisted, and brought up his knee as he pushed Bears head down, making the two meet with a bone splitting thud. Bears stumbled forward and fell on his face, moaning. He slowly rolled to his side, then struggled to rise. Gabe stood, watching, waiting, grinning, and shaking his head. "Stubborn!" he muttered.

Bears searched the ground around for a weapon, spotted his knife and dove for it, but as his outstretched hand grabbed the knife, Gabe's foot bore down on his wrist. Bears twisted and grabbed at Gabe's foot, jerked hard and caused Gabe to stumble backwards, giving Bears space to jump to his feet. Gabe had fallen to his back, but quickly rolled away and rose, just as Bears charged. He stabbed at Gabe's middle, catching the buckskin tunic and ripping it open, but Gabe's iron grip clamped down and kept it from reaching his skin. Gabe stood unmoving, holding Bears wrist, then slowly lifted it away from his tunic, staring at the man's eyes all the while, and showed his strength as he held the wrist against the full force of Bears' lunge. The Comanche looked at him, eyes wide, unbelieving this man could hold him immobile as he did. He stepped back, lowered his shoulder slightly, wanting to drive the knife into Gabe's chest, but as he shifted his weight, Gabe threw himself back, pulling Bears with him, and lifted his knee to Bears chest and tossed Bears over his head to land on his own face, the knife arm beneath him. Bears rolled to the side, and saw blood at his middle, realizing his own knife had cut deeply into his belly. He looked at the wound, glared at Gabe, and struggled to his feet again.

Bears screamed and charged Gabe, fury burning in his eyes, desperation showing in his moves, but Gabe feinted to the left, spun to his right, and grabbed Bears left arm, twisting it as he passed and jerked it from its socket, bone grinding against bone, and with a severe twist, broke the bone below the elbow. Bears screamed at the pain, fell to his knees as he dropped the knife to grab at his distorted arm, tears plowing streaks through the dust on his face, his breath coming in sobs with the pain.

Gabe stepped back, picked up his hawk and stuffed it in his belt, picked up Bears' hawk, walked behind him and picked up his knife. He dropped to one knee before Many Bears and started to speak, when a black streak passed by, the unmistakable growl of Wolf catching Gabe's attention as Wolf drove Crazy Hawk to the ground, his teeth buried in the man's arm that had started to throw a tomahawk at Gabe. When they hit the ground, Wolf shook his head side to side, ripping and tearing Crazy Hawk's arm, the bone cracking under the vice-like bite. Hawk screamed, slapping at Wolf's head, trying to free his arm. It was only at Gabe's shout, that Wolf released the man's arm and stepped back, snarling, and snapping with blood dripping from his teeth.

Cougar Woman shouted, "No!" as Rattling Voice started toward the wolf, hawk upraised, but the shouted warning stopped the man, freezing him in place, looking sideways at Crazy Hawk and Many Bears, neither of whom were looking at him. He looked at Cougar Woman, who stood with her bow at full draw, the arrow pointed at Rattling Voice's chest. He slowly lowered the hawk as Cougar said, "Put it away! Tend to your friends!"

Gabe stepped to Cougar's side, looked down at her and without taking his eyes off the Comanche, "You think we oughta bind 'em up or somethin'?"

Cougar looked up at her man, shook her head and said, "You beat them, break them, bloody them, and you want me to bind them?"

Gabe shrugged, grinned, "I reckon," he chuckled, then added, "I'll help."

It was a disheartened and defeated trio that rode away from their encounter with Gabe and Cougar Woman. Both Many Bears and Crazy Hawk had bandaged arms in splints, Many Bears had many bandages on his face and head, and Rattling Voice was in the lead for the first time in his years as a warrior, having shown courage, although rather limited, for the first time in his life as a Comanche warrior. As they started to leave, Gabe said, "You can tell Old Owl and White Knife we might come to the village soon, but we will come in peace."

Cougar Woman looked at Gabe with a frown, surprised at his words, and wondering just what her man had in mind this time. She shook her head as they watched the three ride to the south, the lowering sun stretching their shadows toward the eastern hills. She looked at Gabe, "You want to go to the village of the Comanche?"

"Yeah, I thought we might take some meat to the women who lost their men, maybe try to make peace with 'em, stop all this fightin' and havin' to watch for the next war party that comes lookin' for vengeance," drawled Gabe as he reached for the lead rope of the big grey. He flipped it over the grey's mane, stroked the neck of the gelding and scratched his forehead, then turned to Cougar Woman. "Why, don't you think it would be good to have peace with 'em?"

"Yes, but if all they want is vengeance, it might not be a good idea to ride into their village, even if we do bring meat for the women who lost their men."

"Hmm, well, we'll think about it a spell, see what Ezra and Dove think of the idea."

Cougar swung aboard her appaloosa, pulled beside Gabe, and shook her head. "You were a little rough on Many Bears, I thought you would just throw him around some and run him off."

"He was too stubborn to run. Needed a little extra encouragement," surmised Gabe as they started back to the cabin and their family.

20 / HUNT

The chicory/coffee blend steamed from the cup as Gabe sipped, looking through the steam at Ezra. The men had just returned from their hilltop prayer times and were enjoying their morning routine of a cup of java as they talked over the day's plans. "So, what'chu think?" asked Gabe, taking another sip of the hot brew.

"'bout what?" asked Ezra, only asking the question to gather his thoughts and come up with a logical answer. He knew what Gabe was inquiring about, and he had thought about the idea of riding uninvited into the village of the Comanche and it just did not sit well with him. The Comanche were known as a warring people and their experience so far had confirmed that reputation. Although they had ridden unbidden into many other villages of tribes from the lands of the east to the far reaches of the wilderness known as

Spanish Louisiana and had lived to tell the story, but the Comanche, well, they were different.

"You know what, visiting the Comanche village."

"Are you really trying to make peace or are you just feeling guilty about makin' so many of their women, widows?"

Gabe breathed deep, turning his gaze to the clearing before the cabin, listening to the morning song of the meadowlark that sat atop the ponderosa. He thought about Ezra's question, considered his motives and concerns, "Maybe a little of both. I know most villages take care of their own, never letting a family do without and such. But, when they lose so many, it makes it hard on the whole village. Granted, it's early in the season and game is plentiful, but they haven't taken any buffalo. Their hunt was stopped when the Mouache Ute had their hunt, and when the war party attacked the Arapaho, they didn't get much."

"Just what were you thinkin' of takin' to the village?"

"Maybe a couple buffalo, an elk or so, whatever we manage to get."

Ezra noisily sipped his java, looked over the rim at Gabe, "I reckon that first fella, White Knife, prob'ly spoke favorable about us, but it didn't stop 'em from gettin' up a couple more war parties to come after us, cuz I think that bunch that hit the 'rapaho were on their way here. And after what you did to those other'ns, Many Bears and his friends, I don't think you made any friends with them. So, what's to keep 'em from comin' again? Or if we go to them, what's to keep 'em from takin' the meat then takin' our scalps?"

"Maybe we could just get near the camp, not go in, but leave the meat an' let 'em know we come in peace."

"And just how you plan on doin' that?"

"Dunno, hafta give it some thought."

"Now, that's a novel idea!" chuckled Ezra. "But I reckon in the meantime, it wouldn't hurt to do a little huntin'."

Gabe looked at his friend, his leg still in splints, fresh bandages on his shoulder and more, "What kind of huntin' do you think you can do?"

Ezra bent forward and slapped his leg, winced, and said, "I'm healin'! I'm healin'!"

"Maybe you could sit here on the porch and I'll try to drive an elk into the clearing yonder so you could shoot him. Then we could get the kids some real sharp knives and let them do the skinnin' and butcherin'!" suggested Gabe, grinning at his friend.

Ezra shook his head, grumbled, "You think you're funny, don'tchu!?"

Gabe finished off his coffee, looked at the dregs in the bottom of the cup, "Come to think of it, we're facing a greater emergency hereabouts, we're 'bout outta coffee!"

"Well, while you and Cougar woman go huntin', me'n Dove and the young'uns will go lookin' for some

chicory, but don't hold out much hope. I ain't seen any
this far west, but we'll go lookin'!"

Gabe rose and went into the cabin to talk to Cougar
about hunting and was surprised when she nodded to
a stack of gear beside the door, "That is what you will
need. I will stay with the children while you hunt."

Gabe looked at his woman, then turned to look
at the stack of gear, a bedroll, his saddle bags, his
rifle, possibles pouch, bow and quiver, saddle pistols, and a small parfleche that bulged at the sides,
probably with foodstuffs packed by Cougar. He
frowned, turned, and asked, "So, you don't wanna
go with me?"

"Yes, but our boys need me too. So, I will stay, and
help Dove with the little ones and the biggest boy of
the bunch," nodding to the porch to include Ezra.

Gabe nodded, grinning, knowing that Cougar
Woman enjoyed being a mother and treasured
times with the boys. But it was more than just being
with them, she used every opportunity to teach the
youngsters skills they would need as they grew older. Already Bobcat had become adept with his bow,
having bagged several rabbits on the run, and she
continually taught the boys about the land, plants,
animals, and more. Seldom did they go into the
woods that Bobcat thought they should be riding,
for he greatly enjoyed his appaloosa yearling and
spent every possible moment with his horse. Gabe

glanced from the gear to the women, "Alright but take a look around every so often just in case some o' them Comanche are still in a vengeful mood!"

The big grey packhorse trailed free rein behind Ebony, the two horses most often constant companions and wherever Ebony went, the grey willingly followed. Gabe pointed the black up the wide canyon between the massive peaks of the Sawatch range, the white cliffs off his right shoulder. The canyon bottom was about seven hundred yards across, carried the white water of the creek crashing over the many boulders as the broad timber covered shoulders of the mountains pushed in against the aspen, alders and cottonwoods that sided the creek. Every break between the mountains carried a run-off stream that formed the alluvial fans on the valley floor, spreading fertile soil into the canyon bottom and forcing the creek to cut its own path down to the lower reaches. Gabe felt dwarfed and even miniscule as he craned to look to the mountain tops, granite crags that stood barren and bald, supporting the blue canopy of the heavens.

The occasional sound of rattling hooves as they ambled on the trail, was magnified by the close confines of the valley bottom, as the stones tumbled from the trail, echoing back from the steep slopes. The heavy shoulders on the south held thick black timber, but the north flanks showed sparse timber and the white

quartz and limestone of the lower cliffs. It was beautiful country, this high country of the Rocky Mountains
that Gabe savored and loved, and in his solitude, he
soaked in the amazing panorama with its myriad of
colors, shapes, and creatures. A rock clattered down
from on high and prompted Gabe to look up to see
a small herd of bighorn sheep scrambling to higher
realms. The big ram paused and looked down at the
intruders to his domain as if daring them to try to
follow. Gabe grinned, waved at the big horned boss of
the bunch and nudged Ebony deeper into the gorge.

As Gabe rode higher into the mountain vale, he remembered the times during the winter when he would
sit by the fire in the lodge of Stone Buffalo, chief of the
Mouache Ute, as he talked about the many winters his
people had spent in the valley. He told of the trail that
Gabe now traveled and that it led to a high mountain
pass that crossed to the eastern slope and the wide
fertile valleys and many lakes that lay in the territory
of the *Weenuchiu* and *Tabeguache* Ute. "The valley of
the Sawatch has much game. The wapiti and bighorns
make the valley their home all year, and there are many
moose, black bear, and grizzly. It is in this valley that
I saw a spirit bear," declared Stone Buffalo, showing a
slight grin at the man he knew as Spirit Bear.

Gabe grinned at the remembrance, but also recalled
that the bear Stone Buffalo saw was an albino black
bear. When Gabe was given the name Spirit Bear,

the name came from a rare beast of the far northern Rockies whose natural color was a dingy white or pale yellow and was thought to be a close relative of the grizzly, but a breed of its own and known as the Spirit Bear. When Sitting Elk, chief of the Arapaho, gave the name to Gabe, he also gifted him a bear claw necklace that had the pale colored fur still on the claws.

Gabe was suddenly brought from his reverie when Wolf stopped, head lowered, and one paw lifted as he growled the warning. Ebony lifted his head high, ears pricked forward and nostrils flaring as he nervously danced to the side, Gabe pulling the rein taut. They had approached the fork in the valley, one branch of the creek coming from the south and a deep canyon, the other tumbling from a wider valley to the west. To the right of the trail, the valley widened, showing a gravelly bottom with random willows, while across the willow lined creek, an expansive and green meadow stretched to the tree line. Standing at a break in the willows was a monster of a grizzly, pawing the air with his front paws, head cocked to the side as his jaw dropped open and a thunderous roar filled the valley that seemed to narrow as the warning of the grizzly sounded. Gabe reached down to stroke the neck of Ebony, felt the grey move alongside, keeping Ebony between him and the bear, and Gabe spoke loud enough for Wolf to hear, "Easy now, easy." Gabe slowly slipped the Ferguson rifle from the case, bringing it to full cock as he brought it to his shoulder. He continued to speak softly to the animals, reassuring them as he watched the big grizz.

The bruin was all of seventy to eighty yards away, standing over nine feet tall as he threatened all intruders, and Gabe knew the big beasts were known for poor eyesight, but there was nothing wrong with their sense of smell. He could tell the bear was trying to identify the smell, but still watched the brush for any movement. Gabe and the horses were partially obscured by the thick willows, and he kept the animals as still as possible, knowing the bear was probably a little confused by the smell of horses, man, and wolf. As they watched, the big bear dropped to all fours, turned away and splashed across the creek. The next glimpse Gabe had of the bear was of his rump disappearing into the far trees and Gabe spoke again, "It's alright, he's gone."

He shook his head, saw Ebony and Wolf relax and look back at him, and he nudged the big stallion forward, choosing to make camp in the south fork and as far away from the bear's domain as possible. He chuckled to himself and spotted a nice clearing just below a thicket of aspen and nudged Ebony toward the trees. He would make camp, maybe look around for some game, although he did not expect to see any with the smell of bear in the air, and then turn in for the night. Tomorrow would be soon enough to bag some meat.

21 / GAME

"Do you smell 'em too?" asked Gabe as he looked at Wolf, who was standing head up, ears forward, looking down the draw to the confluence of the two forks of the mountain stream. Wolf turned his head around, cocked it to the side and looked at Gabe as if answering him in his own unspoken way that made Gabe feel a little bit stupid for asking such a question of the master of the mountains. "Of course you do! What was I thinking?" chuckled Gabe as he gathered up his possibles pouch to hang it over his neck and shoulder, then pick up the Ferguson rifle. "Then, come on, let's go! Those elk aren't gonna wait all day!" His words came softly, muffled by the brush and trees as he padded down the trail, Wolf at his side.

The distinct smell of elk was unmistakable, but Gabe paused and lifted his head to test the winds for any other giveaway scents. The most distinguishable was that of bear or wolverine, but the brisk morning that lay in the valley, the dim blue canopy overhead, told only of the elk, crisp pine, and slightly bitter aspen. Gabe grinned, looked down at Wolf and motioned him forward. He expected to find the elk near the confluence, knowing they probably came from the west fork that held the higher valley that had shown more green. Although the small fork in that valley still carried water, it was far less than the south fork that chuckled its way into the deeper gorge.

The point of the pyramid like ridge pushed into the valley, its northern slope black with thick timber, but the finger was sparsely covered, and the southern edge was bald with lichen covered limestone slide rock. But the angular point that jutted into the bigger valley and the mouth of the gorge, had a ridge of a shoulder that stretched across the narrow valley, making the creek cascade over the steep drop and scattered boulders, the crashing of the waterfall masking the sounds of Gabe's approach. As he crested the slight shoulder, he spotted the elk just below. A big cow, her orange and tan calf at her side, another cow, a young bull with velvet covered spike antlers, and a yearling. Gabe guessed the bull to be maybe three years old, but still hanging around with his mother and last year's calf. The little bunch was stretched out as the trail cut through the willows, giving access to the deeper waters of the creek. Gabe mumbled, "Well, looks like you're gonna hafta make the sacrifice for the womenfolk, mister bull," as he brought the Ferguson to bear on the bull. He slowly eared back the hammer, narrowed his sight, and lightly squeezed the thin forward trigger. The Ferguson, bucked, roared, and spat the bullet through the cloud of grey smoke as Gabe craned to see the big ball strike the bull in the neck, knocking the animal to the ground where his legs kicked out and he let out a short bellow, then lay still. The racketing echo of the blast bouncing across the canyon, scattering birds and little creatures.

The other elk jumped at the shot, stretched out their long dark legs crashing through the willows to cross the stream and turn toward the heavy timber. Gabe watched them scamper away, the gangly calf matching his mother's stride step for step. Within seconds they were gone, and the stillness settled over the valley. It was as if a brief storm had blown through the canyon, rattling leaves, brushing past trees, disturbing the harmonies of the winged chorale and the whispers of the unseen characters on nature's stage. But the softness of silence came again, then an occasional song trotted through the crisp morning air, sent on its way by the colorful bluebird of the treetops, only to be answered by the shrill announcement of the mountain canary that he was ready for the day.

Gabe had naturally reloaded, almost entirely by feel, as he kept his eyes on the downed elk, and satisfied it was dead, he rose from his half crouch, stood to look over the currant bushes, then parted the brush and walked down the slight slope to the carcass. Wolf trotted before him and stood beside the carcass as Gabe came near. "So, you gonna help me dress him out, are ya?" asked Gabe, grinning at his furry friend.

Wolf cocked his head to the side, appearing to frown at Gabe, then lazily stretched out under the willows to await his share of the innards, what he probably thought was the best part. Gabe worked hard at the task, skinning out the carcass and deboning all the meat, wanting to make as compact a bundle in the hide as possible. Although many other parts, sinew, guts, tongue, and more, were usually put to use, Gabe was interested only in the meat and hide. Once he completed his task, he put the bundle of meat under the overhanging willows, away from the gut pile and bones, looked at Wolf who appeared satisfied with his feast of scraps and more, "You watch this! I'm goin' after the horses and I'll be right back."

Gabe looked at Wolf, turned away and started back up the trail. The rigging of the horses, packing up the camp, and returning to the kill site took about a half hour, but Gabe was surprised when he pushed through the brush at the crest of the shoulder to look below. Three wolves were fanned out, facing Wolf and the meat bundle. But Wolf was standing his ground, head lowered, teeth showing, watching the beasts before him. It was obvious Wolf was larger than any of the others, probably outweighing the largest by at least thirty pounds, and standing about six inches taller at the shoulder. Yet the three before him were like beasts of every breed, four legged and two legged, thinking there is strength in numbers and that they had the advantage, an advantage none of them would have if they were alone.

Gabe watched only for a second, then dug heels to Ebony and charged the scene, screaming and shouting as he drew one of the saddle pistols and brought it to full cock as he neared the wolfpack. He took a quick aim at the largest of the three, a grey male with hackles raised and teeth showing as he turned to face the new threat. Gabe dropped the hammer, saw the bullet raise dust on the heavy coat and the wolf stagger, then turn away, tail tucked between his legs as he stumbled into the brush, following the other two that gave way almost immediately.

Gabe brought Ebony to a sliding stop, threw his leg over the black's neck, and dropped to the ground, facing the brush where the pack disappeared, watching for any to show itself. But the brush did not move, and Gabe felt the familiar fur of Wolf brush his leg as his friend sided him, also looking at the brush. Gabe reached down to run his fingers through Wolf's scruff, "Good boy! You did good! Just like I asked!"

The big grey packhorse had followed Ebony

through the willows and now stood beside the stallion, both watching Gabe and Wolf as they returned to the meat bundle. Gabe soon had the bundle secured on the pack saddle cross bucks and stepped aboard Ebony. He glanced at Wolf and with a wave of his hand, they started into the canyon, pointed towards home.

The sun had yet to bend its rays into the bottom of the canyon, still lingering behind the tall eastern peaks, but the day was clear and bright. They kept to the trail on the north side of the creek, until the stream made a dog leg bend around a point of a shoulder of the big mountain on the south side, that brought them face to face with the brilliant but warm sun that seemed to be cradled between the two peaks at the mouth of the canyon. Gabe shielded his eyes, Ebony dropped his head, and Wolf padded on paying little attention to the high sun. A clatter of rocks off his left shoulder brought Gabe to a stop and he leaned away from the slope to look up the steep talus to see a herd of big horn sheep starting up the steep slope away from the creek.

Gabe grabbed the Ferguson, swung down from the saddle, and stood spread-legged in the trail, resting his left triceps against his rib cage to steady his aim, he brought the sights to bear on a mature ram, but not the herd ram. It was about half way up the first bit of a climb, in the middle of the herd, when Gabe's rifle roared. The ram stumbled, rolled to the side, and tumbled down hill, coming to rest in a heap about ten feet below the trail.

Gabe instantly spun the trigger guard, opening the breech, tucked the ball and patch in the breech, grabbed his powder horn and loaded the opening, spinning the trigger guard to close the breech and then filled the pan, snapped the frizzen down, bringing the hammer to full cock as he lifted the rifle for another shot. Another ram, near the end of the line paused to look below, and never took another step. He faltered in his step, stumbled, and fell to the side, the rest of the herd moving quickly past.

Gabe was reloading as he watched the others climb the almost sheer cliff face, bounding from one cleft to another, moving like they had glue on their hooves, none hesitating as they fled, and the entire herd was soon beyond his sight. Gabe breathed deep, looked around, saw Wolf looking at him and waiting, then he slipped the rifle back into the scabbard, reached to his belt and touched the butt of his over/under Bailes pistol for reassurance, then started up the trail to retrieve the two carcasses.

When Gabe came into the clearing by the cabin, he was walking, leading Ebony and the grey following close behind. The two bundles of meat of the bighorns were aboard Ebony, while the grey carried the meat bundle of the elk. Wolf walked beside Gabe as he waved to Ezra who was struggling to stand from his seat on the porch. Gabe grinned at Ezra, "Have you even moved since I left?"

"Nope. Been waitin' for you to drive that Elk from the trees so I could shoot him!" answered Ezra, grinning at his friend. "I didn't expect you to already have him skinned and gutted for me!"

"Well, I got to thinkin' 'bout the young'uns trying to do all that bloody work with sharp knives and what Cougar might say about her kids havin' to do that kinda work, so I figgered it'd be better all around if I just went ahead an' done it!"

"Good thinkin'!" declared Ezra, taking it slow as he descended the steps from the porch, the crutch under his arm.

Cougar and Dove came through the doorway, stood on the porch, and watched as Gabe came near. Cougar quickly went to his side, embraced her man, and stepped back to look at the bundles of meat. "I'll start a fire, you unload, we'll smoke it right away."

"You're not going to cut it and smoke it are you?"
"No, but we will smoke the big pieces to keep it until you take it to the Comanche."

Gabe frowned, wondering how she always seemed to know what he was going to do even before he did, but he just shook his head and did as he was told, grinning at the thought.

From his prayer perch atop the long finger ridge behind and above the cabin, Gabe sat on his familiar rock and looked to the east as the first light of day began its push against the retreating darkness. The lone distant peak clung to the hem of darkness as the thin line a blue made silhouettes of the nearer line of hills. A long streak of clouds scarred the sky, appearing as a hem on the garment of night, but the rising sun began to paint the underbellies a dim shade of pink. Gabe leaned back against the trunk of the lone ponderosa and smiled at the wonder of God's creation.

He stood, watching the colors of the sunrise, turned away and started back to the cabin. This day would be challenging at best and deadly at worst, but he put his trust in his Lord, believing what he planned to do was the right thing. Because of his splint and crutch, Ezra was limited in his access to his usual promontory of prayer and chose instead to stay porch bound and do his praying from the rocking chair. As Gabe and Wolf came around the corner of the house, Ezra greeted him with a question, "You still set on goin'?"

"Yeah, I just can't shake the feelin' that it's what I oughta do!" answered Gabe as he sat on the top step of the porch, watching the rising sun paint the white cliffs with shades of pink. He twisted around to look at his friend, "I'd rather be goin' with you, but since you took flyin' lessons from that bull buffalo, you ain't fit for much!"

"If you could wait a few days, mebbe a week, I'd prob'ly be healed up 'nuff to go with you!"

"If I waited any longer, I'd prob'ly talk myself out of it!"

"Ain't no harm in that! Reckon it'd be safer dealin' with your conscience than them Comanche!"

Gabe chuckled, shook his head, and rose to go into the cabin. He heard the women puttering around and wanted to get his gear ready, anticipating an early departure. Cougar met him as he came in, nodded to the stack of gear by the door, smiling. "I just can't get ahead of you can I?" he drawled as he drew her close for an embrace. He held her tight just as their youngest, Fox, bounced off his mother as he rubbed the sleep from his eyes. She reached down and picked up the two-year-old, gave him a hug and yielded to his squirming to get down. She laughed as he toddled away in search of the other youngsters.

Cougar leaned into her man, "Do you think you will be gone long?"

Gabe cocked his head to the side, frowned, "Oh, it'll be a day gettin' there, another day back, maybe a day or two there, so hopefully, less'n a week."

"I do not like you doing this alone," she started, but was interrupted by Gabe.

"I know, but," he paused, looking at the youngsters playing together in the far corner of the cabin, "I'd rather have you here with them, you know," he declared, leaving the rest unsaid but understood.

Cougar reached behind her, turned, and held the grizzly claw necklace before her, motioning for him to bend down to let her slip it over his head. As it dropped into place, she touched it, looked up at her man and kissed him.

As Gabe rode from the clearing, Wolf was trotting beside him and the big grey packhorse trailed behind carrying the four bundles of meat, two of the elk and two bighorns, and a parfleche and pack with trade goods. The sun was about two fingers above the eastern horizon and shone bright upon the green valley before him. He took the trail that angled over the long finger ridge after working its way through the sweet-smelling pines and the random patches of aspen. He crested the ridge and pointed Ebony to the southwest to cross the long wide valley toward the mouth of the canyon that carried the Arkansa river through the foothills of the Sangre de Cristo range.

It was just past mid-day when he started across the river, just upstream of the anthill shaped hillock that lay on the north side of the river. The gravel bottomed crossing was easy enough with the water belly deep on both Ebony and the dapple-grey packhorse. Wolf paddled his way across, climbed the bank and stood to shake his heavy fur, rolling his coat, and scattering water everywhere. Ebony and the grey stopped near the big wolf, and Gabe had just stepped down when Ebony shook and rolled his skin, wanting to roll in the grass but hindered by the saddle and gear. He looked at Gabe as if asking for relief, but none was coming and both horses had to be satisfied with their shaking to rid their coats of the excess water.

Gabe had tried to escape from the deluge of animals shaking but failed to make his escape and stood before them, buckskins dripping with cast off water, as he shook his head at the three. "Just had to gang up on me, didn'tchu!?" as he tried to wipe some of the excess away. He shook his head, stepped back aboard the black and nudged him to the trail that sided the river. When the river pushed closer to the long talus slope to make a wide bend, Gabe chose the grassy bank and shore to make his mid-day stop. He stepped down, loosened the cinches of the saddle and packsaddle, led the horses to the water and once they were satisfied, he ground tied them on the grass and sought out a shady spot beside a scraggly alder for his own snack.

It was late afternoon when he saw the well-used trail fork and the more recent tracks showing a river crossing. He looked downstream and saw the canyon mouth and chose to follow the tracks to cross to the south side of the river. As he neared the mouth of the canyon, he turned into a gulch that lay at the base of a hog back ridge timbered with thick juniper and piñon. He pushed into the gulch until he was well obscured from the canyon, tethered the horses, and loosened the girths. With telescope in hand and Wolf at his side, he started the climb to the crest of the hog back.

At the crest, the hogback had a slight saddle, sided on both ends by rim rock and spotted with stunted piñon. Gabe chose his promontory beside the big rocks and sat in the shade of a tree as he withdrew the scope. He already spotted the village of the Comanche which lay less than a mile away on the far side of a wide flat that was shouldered by a long mesa on the south, the hogbacks on the north, the river to the east and the mountains to the west. It was the perfect setting for a village, well protected from the weather, easily defended with flats all around, and good observation atop the long mesa on the south.

He stretched out the brass tube, used his knees to support his elbows and steady the scope, and began his survey of the village. It was too far to identify anyone, but he could watch the activity and get an idea of the lay of the village, the location of the leaders' lodges, and more. It was a sizeable village, maybe thirty lodges, which meant they could field about seventy or seventy-five warriors or hunters. The loss of ten or more warriors would be a hardship for the people, for almost every warrior would leave a woman and/or family the people would have to provide for and protect, making a burden on the others. But the remaining fifty or sixty warriors would still be a formidable force.

As he watched, he saw a hunting party of about six or seven come from the river, well downstream of where he crossed, and they had several deer across their horses' rumps. Another group came from the long draw that fell from the high mountains, but only one horse carried game. *Not a lot of meat for prob'ly a hundred, hundred fifty people,* thought Gabe, watching as the hunters dropped meat before several lodges, probably their own. He kept a close watch on the activity and saw a handful of women together, watching as the meat was distributed but receiving none. The women turned away, all going to lodges that were on the uphill side of the encampment, and Gabe mentally marked each lodge that showed no sign of a man. He identified four lodges in close proximity to each other, where women gathered but no men showed.

Gabe lowered the scope to search the countryside for possible approaches to the Comanche encampment. He glanced at the sky, saw the sun was lowering over the Sangre de Cristo mountain range that lay to the southeast of the lodges and guessed there to be about an hour's daylight left. Of course dusk held ample light for traveling, and if he remembered correctly the moon was waxing full. He eyeballed the terrain, noted the gulch below the hogback continued toward the mountains, paralleled another that led closer to the timbered foothills. From there he could move around the upper end of the village and maybe approach it with cover along the creek that appeared to split the encampment. He grinned, then lifted the scope for a more thorough scan of the village and the activity of the people.

If they were to expect an attack, the obvious approach would be from the river and that end would be closely watched. The uphill side was against the tree line of the foothills, well covered, and easily protected. No one would expect an attack or an encroachment from the higher foothills and mountains beyond. *But do I do it under cover of night, sneak in and leave. Or do I ride in during sunlight hours? That one hothead, Many Bears, no tellin' what he'd do, or try to do. He would want to stir the others up against me, then what?*

Gabe shook his head, still watching the lodges, when movement caught his attention. One of the central lodges had a gathering before it, several men were close in and appeared to be arguing, uplifted hands, restless movement. *I wonder what that's all about?* considered Gabe as he watched. One man stepped forward, arms uplifted, and the others moved back, and at the motion of the one, the rest seated themselves. Three men stood before the lodge, one man was obviously speaking, gesturing, and looking at the others as he moved side to side. He, apparently finished, stepped back and the second man began speaking. This went on for several minutes, then the crowd dispersed, and the three speakers ducked into the big lodge.

Gabe watched until the light faded, then slipped the scope back into the case and with Wolf at his side, returned to the gulch where the horses were tethered. As he walked, he thought, undecided about what would be best, to either enter the camp under cover of darkness, or wait until morning and ride in without any cover, exposed for all to see. He shook his head as he returned the scope to the saddle bags and dug some smoked meat from the other side and sat down to think and chew on the meat. He looked at Wolf, "So, what do you think? Tonight or tomorrow?"

Wolf looked up at Gabe, accepted a tossed piece of

meat, and lowered his head between his paws as he chewed on the meat. "You're no help!" declared Gabe, chasing the furtive answer through the recesses of his mind, knowing this was something he needed to trust the Lord about and the best way to do that was to spend a little time in prayer.

23 / CONSIDERATION

Gabe guessed it to be about an hour shy of midnight when he pointed Ebony up the draw. The sandy bottom accumulated over years of snow melt runoff made movement as quiet as a snake slithering across the sand. Hooves pushed into the sand, each step no more than a whisper. Gabe glanced at the moon that stood over his left shoulder, waxing full and giving the familiar hushed blue tint to the terrain. They were moving as much by feel as by sight with the banks of the draw about fifty feet above them, but as they gained ground, the gulch grew shallow and the intermittent piñon and scrub juniper masked their movements. Once at the head of the gulch, he crossed over a slight saddle to the parallel draw to continue toward the foothills below the Sangre de Cristo mountains.

Within moments he neared the pinnacle rock he

picked as a landmark from his earlier scan of the countryside. He paused, pushed Ebony to the crest of the low ridge, stood in his stirrups for a looksee, then nudged the black into the shadows of the timber covered ridge and on into the wider draw to cross the trickle of a stream and move back into the thicker trees. He reined up and stepped down, walked to the tree line for another surveillance of the camp. He remembered what he had impressed on his mind about the lay of the land and the location of the Comanche camp, knowing there was a ragged ridge that pushed close to the upper end of the camp, but another long finger ridge sided the camp to the south, however, he reckoned there would be lookouts on that ridge.

His tentative plan was to enter the village in the wee hours of the morning, while most were in their deepest sleep, and leave the bundles of meat outside the lodges he marked as those of the women alone and probably the widows of the warriors he killed. Then come morning, he would approach the village in the full light of day, to make peace talk, without them thinking he was trying to buy their favor with the offered meat, an act that some natives would consider to be a sign of weakness. As he looked at the camp below, a sudden flash of light caught his attention. He looked to the south, saw a bolt of lightning travel its ragged path from the clouds to the ground, followed soon after by the deep throated rumble of thunder.

Between the camp and an inset notch in the long ridge, the horse herd of the Comanche restlessly milled about with the sound of the coming storm. There was little movement in the camp except by a few restless horses tethered beside the lodge of their owners. It was common for warriors to keep their favorite hunting or war horse near their lodge, tending to their needs personally and strengthening the bond between horse and rider. Gabe glanced at the moon, then to the approaching storm clouds, timed the space between the lightning and thunder and calculated the storm to be less than two miles away. Another glance to the moon and he made his decision. He would use the cover of the storm to accomplish his task.

He swung back aboard Ebony and crossed the ragged ridge to begin working closer to the camp, using the ridge as cover. Within a short while, he was at the end of the ridge and just inside the tree line. The end of the ridge was marked by a low timber covered flat topped knob, and across the little creek to the north and a little further down the wide draw, another almost bald knob stood marking the upper end of the village. From Gabe's position, the upper end of the Comanche camp and the lodges of the women was about four hundred yards, but he could use the brush beside the creek to mask his approach. With the four bundles of meat, two of the elk and the two bighorns, atop the grey, he would walk into the camp, leading the grey, drop the bundles before the women's lodges, and return, hopefully unseen and unheard.

After checking the bundles and loosely tethering Ebony in the shelter of a juniper, he motioned Wolf to stay with the Black and watched as the wolf bellied down and stretched out, big eyes watching his friend. Gabe replaced his Bailes belt pistol, with both saddle pistols. The French saddle pistols were heavier, but double barreled and the locks were water tight. The Bailes was double barreled, but to fire the second round, the barrels had to be rotated to the hammer, while the saddle pistols had double locks and if needed, both barrels could be fired at once, dropping both hammers simultaneously. He tightened his sash to secure the pistols, slipped the tail his tunic up and over to protect them, then grabbed the lead rope of the grey and started into the night.

As he walked, he felt his chin, relieved he had shaved before leaving the cabin, as was his usual habit, although occasionally he would let his chin whiskers grow. But he wanted a clean face as he went into the camp, whiskers would be a giveaway that the shadowy figure of the night was not a Comanche. He had no sooner sided the creek than the first drops of rain pelted his face. It was a heavy rain, the kind that could bring flash floods down a creek like this one, but that would take a while and he planned on being done with his drop off before that happened.

As he neared the first lodge, the downpour was coming at a slant, driven by the wind that came over the ridge. The steady beat of rain on the hide lodges was like a distant drummer beating a constant rhythm for a dance, Gabe thought, *Must be for a rain dance!* And chuckled to himself. He stopped before the first lodge, untied the bundle of bighorn and sat it before the entry. Nothing and no one moved, no sound came from the lodge, and Gabe moved to the next one. He stopped, stripped off the second bundle, dropped it beside the entry, and moved away. As he led the grey toward the next lodge, the big horse's hoof clattered against a tipi peg, giving a slight shake to the lodge. A startled cry came from within and Gabe heard movement, a few words mumbled, and Gabe quickly led the grey away from the entry to stop slightly beyond. He stripped off the first bundle of elk meat and hide, started toward the lodge when the entry flap was thrown back and the light from the interior fire stabbed into the darkness. The sizable figure of a woman, bent through the entry, looking around and spoke, "You! What are you doing in the rain?" Her words and manner said she was a figure used to command.

Gabe was fluent in the tongue of the Shoshoni and the language of the Comanche was much the same, but he knew to say too much could be a giveaway. He stood on the far side of the grey, away from the light, the bundle heavy in his hands and he growled, "Meat!" and sat the bundle down at the edge of the shaft of light, then started away. He glanced back to see the woman step into the rain, her attention focused on the meat, grab the bundle, and turn back to her lodge without another word or look his way.

The last lodge he visually and mentally marked, was just ahead and he continued in the heavy downpour. As he walked beside the grey, he loosened the straps securing the last bundle and without stopping, dropped the bundle beside the entry and moved into the darkness. He breathed a heavy sigh, relieved he had not been stopped, and started toward the ridge and the trees where Ebony waited. He sloshed through the mud, the grey's hooves plopping and sucking in the clay like mire, until he was about fifty yards from the line of lodges, and he heard some shouting and other ruckus. He looked over the back of the grey to see a torch before one of the lodges and heard some shouting that he was certain came from the big woman that had confronted him.

He and the grey stood unmoving, watching, knowing their image was obscured by the thickets of brush beside the creek and any sign of their passing would soon be obliterated by the deluge. Within moments, the ruckus subsided, the torch disappeared and quiet settled over the camp as the rain lessened and the clouds covered the moon.

Gabe relaxed and resumed their jaunt to the trees to rejoin Ebony and Wolf, both of whom were probably just as wet as him and the grey.

When he came to Ebony, he quickly swung aboard and reined the black over the low saddle crossing of the ridge to a heavy thicket of cottonwoods that would afford better cover from the last of the rain and be well out of sight of the camp. He hoped it would be possible to get a small fire going to dry off and maybe get a little something to eat before daylight and his journey to circle around and approach the camp. But first things first, it was time to get dry and warm up a mite.

24 / MEETING

The first grey light was timidly showing itself as Gabe started across the little creek, bound for the same trail he followed from the river. His plan was to return to his promontory lookout, scan the village and terrain, then go to the encampment to meet the Comanche. He had spent his usual time in prayer, but he was still a little uneasy. He took his time through the trees, dropped into the long sandy bottomed gulch, and pushed toward the rising sun.

He gave Ebony his head and checked the loads on his weapons as he rocked with the easy gait of the stallion. Wolf was trotting before them, an occasional glance over his shoulder to be sure they were still following and ducked under an overhanging branch from a crooked leaning cottonwood. Wolf suddenly stopped, lowered his head, and let a low growl crawl from his chest. Ebony stopped. Gabe leaned forward

shading his eyes from the bright sun that was splitting the horizon directly in front of him but saw
nothing. He stepped down, rifle in hand, and slowly
searched the nearby trees for any movement, but
everything was still. No morning breeze, no early
rising songbirds, no late returning bats, nothing.
Gabe glanced at Ebony who stood, head up, ears
forward, as much because of what Wolf was doing
as at anything that alarmed him.

Gabe turned back toward the mouth of the draw,
saw a flitting but unidentifiable shadow, glanced at
Wolf but the beast paid no attention. He was focused
on the small clearing where Gabe had tethered the
horses the day before, and slowly padded toward
the trees. Gabe hung back, watching his friend. Wolf
approached the site, dropped his nose to sniff the area,
lifted his head to look around, then looked at Gabe as
if to say, "Well, come on!"

Gabe started slowly forward, still searching the
trees, the rein from Ebony hanging loosely over his
arm and the animals trailing behind. Gabe looked
down at Wolf, "So, what'd you smell boy?" and looked
around the small clearing. He dropped to one knee
and touched the ground where the faint trace of a
moccasin track overlapped the hoofprints of his horses. Someone was here after they left late last night. He
looked around, trying to determine when the visitor
had been there and if there were more. As he looked,

touching the ground around, looking at the grasses and the sign, he was puzzled. The tracks showed only one man, and that he was here after Gabe left, but it was late last night. The dew on the grasses around had not been disturbed and an early morning scout would have left more sign.

As he rose, he looked around for any other indication of visitors, but saw nothing. He relaxed, tethered the horses, and with scope in hand and Wolf at his side, he climbed the hogback for another good survey of the encampment. What he saw was the usual early morning activity of any village; women busy at cookfires, rambunctious children wanting to play, men and others making their usual morning visit to the bushes and trees, nothing unusual. With another slow scan of the entire camp and the nearby area, Gabe was satisfied and with Wolf at his side, returned to the horses.

He stroked the neck of Ebony, talked to him as he ran his fingers through his mane, "Well, boy, we're about to ride into the devil's lair and there's no tellin' what we're gonna find! I'm trustin' you to stay calm," he paused and looked down at Wolf, "and *you* to be watchful." He stepped to the side of the grey, stroked his neck, and spoke softly to him, knowing all the while he was trying to still his own nerves. Gabe shook his head, chuckling as he swung aboard the big stallion and started from the gulch.

Gabe sat tall in the saddle, as he ran his fingers through his blonde hair that hung to his shoulders. He had put his usual floppy felt hat in the bedroll wanting the first impression of the white man to be as impressive as possible. Gabe knew he was an impressive figure, form fitting beaded buckskins, grizzly bear claw necklace, long hair, broad shoulders, and weapons everywhere. He stood just over six foot tall, weighed about one ninety-five, and was lithe in his movements and confident in his manner, while his eyes showed mischief and friendliness. As he neared the encampment, he breathed deep and watched for any sign of being seen.

A shout sounded, people moved about, a couple of youngsters stood staring and pointing until a handful of armed warriors stepped forward, lined out as if to block his entry to the camp and one man stepped forward. Gabe held up his right hand, palm forward, and left hand held the reins slightly to the side so the men could see he held no weapons. Gabe spoke, "I come in peace! I am Spirit Bear, friend of the Comanche White Knife." He reined up about ten feet before the leader of the warriors who scowled at him and tossed his head as if to say, "Scram!" but Gabe sat still, waiting.

Wolf had trailed beside Ebony, hanging off his right flank and watching the warriors. Gabe spoke, "I come in peace to see White Knife. I am Spirit Bear."

"He is the one that killed our brothers!" screamed a

man from behind the line of warriors. Gabe frowned, looked at the man who was hidden by the warrior in front, but Gabe leaned to the side to see Rattling Voice. Gabe grinned, "Rattling Voice! You made it back without getting lost or running away!"

The man snarled and dropped his eyes, turning away. But the words of Gabe brought laughter from some of those in the line who knew Rattling Voice. The laughter relaxed the mood of the warriors and the leader asked, "Why do you come to our village?"

"As I said, I come to see White Knife. I hope to speak with his father, Old Owl, and talk peace between our people."

"Aiieeee!" screamed another, "He is the ghost that came in the night with meat!" The scream came from a large woman and after her words, Gabe guessed her to be the woman by the lodge that saw him in the rain. "That horse!" she shouted, "carried the bundles of meat! It is a ghost horse!" she screamed and turned to toddle away as fast as her girth would allow.

The crowd had increased with several women and children and additional warriors when a youngster about ten summers pointed and shouted, "LOOK! He has a wolf!" and quickly went behind his mother, grabbing at her tunic. Chatter started among the crowd, some pointing and talking, others drawing back and whispering.

The warning from the boy made the warriors

look beside the big stallion and spotting Wolf, they stepped back and looked from the beast to the man. Gabe said, "He is my friend," and motioned Wolf forward to stand beside Ebony's front leg. The warriors watched wide-eyed, awed by the sight of the wolf, and that he could stand beside the man's horse and the horse pay no attention.

The commotion had brought many others and at the back of the crowd, the people began to part as others pushed forward. Gabe recognized White Knife, his arm still bandaged, as he stepped forward, an older man close behind. "Spirit Bear! It is good that you have come as you said you would." He turned to the older man, looked back at Gabe, "This is my father, Old Owl."

The older man stood proudly, arms across his chest, and glared at the brazen intruder to his village and motioned him to step down. The village leader glanced at the wolf, looked at the fine horse, then turned his attention to the white man. "My son has told me of his time with you. You gave my son back to me when you could have made him cross over. For that I am thankful."

"Your son is a good and brave man. He did not deserve to die."

"And the others?"

"They could have lived if they listened when I warned them, but they chose to fight."

"And those that rode with Many Bears?"

"They were warned. I told them to leave and they could live, but Many Bears chose to fight. They had more than one chance to leave, but he would not let them. It was only after we fought, that he chose to return to your village."

"This is true," came the words from someone behind the chief.

Gabe looked past the chief to see Crazy Hawk beside a woman and a child. He nodded to the man and turned his attention back to Old Owl. "I have come in peace. I did not ask for these fights, but I will not run from any man. These men threatened my home, my horses, and my life. I did nothing more than what you would do when your family and home is threatened."

"Come," said Old Owl as he turned away to push through the crowd. Gabe started to follow, and the people crowded back as Wolf walked beside him. As they walked through the village, the people stood looking at the man and his wolf. A boy of about eight or nine summers, dropped to his knees beside wolf and reached out to touch him. Wolf looked up at Gabe, saw him nod, then turned to lick the boy's face just before the boy buried his face in the deep scruff of Wolf's neck. Gabe looked up at the frightened mother, smiled, and said, "I have two sons and Wolf loves to play with them."

The woman nodded, looked at her boy, and

reached to touch his shoulder, "Long Bow, come!" The boy hugged the wolf again, then stood and went to his mother. Gabe grinned and followed after Old Owl and White Knife. As they approached the large central tipi, the chief motioned to White Knife who offered, "Let me take your horses. I will tether them behind the lodge. My father wishes to talk with you."

Gabe nodded and handed off the reins and lead line to the pack horse, but motioned Wolf to stay beside him. Old Owl dropped to his knees on a blanket, twisted around to lean back against a willow back rest and motioned Gabe to be seated close beside him. Gabe sat down cross-legged, motioned to Wolf to lay beside him, and looked to the chief.

"I heard you tell the woman you have sons. How old?"

"The oldest, Bobcat, has seen almost four summers, and the youngest, Fox, is in his second summer."

The old man nodded, frowned and asked, "My son said your woman was a war leader of the Shoshone. She must be a big and mean woman to be a war leader!"

Gabe chuckled, "She's only mean when she needs to be. She did take a little training, but she is a good woman and a great warrior, and beautiful to look upon."

The old man chuckled, nodding, and understanding. "There are others in your camp?"

"My brother, Black Buffalo, and his woman, Grey Dove, who is also Shoshone."

The leader turned his head and looked at Gabe, "Why are you here in this land?"

Gabe grinned, breathed deep, and began, "Since we were boys, the size of the one who petted my wolf, my brother and I longed to come to the great blue mountains, to explore the wild lands, meet the many peoples that live in this great place, to know all that the great Creator had made."

"Have you met many people?" asked the chief.

Gabe grinned, nodded, "We met many. The great Osage, the Missouri, the Otoe, the Pawnee, Omaha, Sioux, Blackfoot, Crow, Coeur d'Alene, Nez Perce, Shoshone, Arapaho, Cheyenne, Mouache Ute, Yamparika Ute, and more. And now the great Comanche." Gabe had watched the leader's reaction to the many names, frowning at some, nodding at others. When Gabe finished, he looked at the leader, waiting for a response.

"I do not know all these names." He paused, looked up at Gabe, "You have met all these?"

"And more. There are many other tribes beyond the great river and more to the far north. This is a big world, my friend."

The chief appeared to have just noticed the claw necklace and he frowned, nodded toward it, and asked, "Did you kill that bear?"

Gabe touched the claws, nodded, "Yes, but it was not easy. He almost killed me!" and grinned.

The chief smiled, laughed, and asked, "Is that how you were named?"

"No, I was given my name by a great chief named Sitting Elk, because I fought beside him and his men against the Pawnee. He said I fought like the Spirit Bear with hair this color," running his fingers through his own hair, "and gave me the name Claw of the Bear or Spirit Bear."

Old Owl frowned, "Sitting Elk? I have fought against that man. He is a great warrior."

"That was many summers ago, before I took a wife and had a family," explained Gabe.

White Knife returned, seated himself, just as the women started serving the men. White Knife explained, "This is my mother, Red Otter, and," nodding to the other woman by the fire, "My woman, Little Rabbit."

Gabe nodded to the women, accepted a trencher loaded with food, and as the others did, he began eating, pleased with the visit, and hoping they would continue in peace.

25 / VISIT

Gabe rolled from his blankets at the touch of a cold nose on his cheek. He looked at the black shadow of Wolf before him, glanced around at the hide lodge where he slept, remembering White Knife directing him to this lodge for the night. "The woman of this lodge will be with her friend who also lost her man. They will prepare a morning meal for you and then we will visit," explained White Knife before he left the lodge. Gabe sat up remembering the time spent with Old Owl as they talked of the many other nations of natives that Old Owl had not known, and they spoke of the men who rode with Many Bears against the Arapaho and to go against Gabe and his family. Old Owl explained, "Our people believe that warriors must earn honors to become the man a woman would want, and the man our people need to lead them in time of war and hunting. Our young men are anxious to earn these honors in battle and on the hunts. To return with bounty, horses, and captives gives them great rewards, it proves they can provide for a family of their own. The man who cannot do this, will never have a woman of his own or a family and is not a man."

"Young men that are hopeful of these honors will follow anyone and often make the wrong choices. Our people believe each man should make his own decisions and answer for them."

Gabe remembered responding, "It is not so different among our people and others. Did we not do the same when we were young?" He grinned at the remembrance, and stood, stretched, and flipped the entry blanket back to exit the lodge. The first light was showing over the tops of the tipis, each tripod of poles seemingly scratching the grey sky as it pushed back the darkness. Wolf was at his side as he walked to the trees for his morning constitutional and to retreat for a time of prayer with his Maker.

Gabe returned to the lodge to find two women busy at the cookfire preparing a meal. White Knife sat on the blanket before the lodge and nodded as Gabe sat down. White Knife motioned to the women, "These are women who lost their men in recent battles." He gestured toward one, "That is Red Face, the other is Walking Bird. They tell of finding packs of meat at their lodge that was left during the storm in the darkness. It is the same as the woman that said you were a ghost with a ghost horse."

Gabe looked up at White Knife, "It is a good thing they have meat, is it not?"

"It is. They have no one to hunt for them and they depend on others now," explained Knife, looking at Gabe for some reaction or sign that would tell of his doing, but Gabe remained stoic, watching the women at work.

"After we eat, we will walk. I would learn more of the ways of the white man and his woman, the Shoshone war leader."

"And I would learn more of the Comanche," replied Gabe, accepting the offered carved wooden trencher of food from Walking Bird.

"My father's father told of people that came from another land and wore shirts and tops," gesturing to his chest and head, "of iron. They were the first to have horses, what some called elk-dogs, and my people traded with them. There have been others we call Comancheros that come from the south and bring trade goods. It is said they speak the same tongue as those with iron shirts. But you are the first of your kind to come among my people. Your hair, the color of dry grass, your skin that is the color of the early morning clouds, and it changes like the color of those clouds in the morning."

Gabe chuckled as he thought of the times his skin had shown almost a bright pink when he had spent too much time in the sun, especially on a cold wintry morning when the wind seemed to cut his face. White Knife's description was vivid and real.

"Are there many of your people?" asked White Knife.

Gabe thought a moment, then explained, "Like the many natives of different people but all the same skin, there are many people of this color," pinching the skin at his wrist, "that are not of the same people. Like you, the Comanche, and your enemy, the Arapaho, you may have the same color of skin, but you are not the same people."

"Are there many people of your color?" persisted White Knife.

"Yes, there are many, but they are far away beyond the great river."

"I have heard of a great river, but I have not seen such a thing. Tell me."

Gabe grinned, gathered his thoughts, and began, "Many of the rivers that you know, this one," pointing to the Arkansa in the valley below, the river that would one day be known as the Arkansas, "the big rivers to the far north that some know as the Missouri, and the Platte rivers, and more, all flow into the great river called the Mississippi. That river comes from the far north and flows into the great waters far to the south.

In places that river is as wide as this valley and as deep as these hills."

He looked at Gabe with a frown that showed more than a little skepticism then asked, "And your friend, Black Buffalo, his skin is as the night sky, and you say you are brothers. How is this so?"

"Even though we had different mothers and fathers, we have been close friends since we were young," he held his hand waist high to indicate the size of a child, "and did everything together. Our families had no other sons, and we called ourselves brothers from the times we spent in the woods, learning about life. We have been together all this time and he *is* my brother."

They walked side by side, letting the trail and time dictate their thoughts until White Knife paused, looked at Gabe and asked, "Why did you let me live and have your woman tend my wound?"

Gabe glanced at the man, "You were not a threat to me. You were wounded. I had no reason to kill you."

"But I tried to steal your horses and I would have killed you if I could," declared Knife, frowning, and shaking his head.

"I know among your people a warrior gains honor when he kills an enemy and takes his horse and goods and scalp. Because to kill an enemy is to help your people and keep that enemy from attacking you sometime. But," he paused, looked at the camp nestled in the valley below them, "I get no pleasure or honor in killing another. I only do that when there is no other way. I have nothing to prove, for it has already been shown that I am a warrior and will fight when I must. I would gain nothing by taking your horse or scalp, I do not need that. When you were no longer a threat to me and my family, then you did not need to die. It is better to have you as a friend than an enemy."

White Knife frowned, glancing at Gabe and Wolf, thinking about what was said, as they continued on the trail that circumvented the camp of the Comanche. After giving White Knife some time to consider what had been said, Gabe asked, "If you had been killed, what then?"

White Knife scowled, his brow furrowed and his eyes dark, "What then?"

"Yes. What do you believe happens, if anything, after you die?" Gabe watched as White Knife considered the question, then added, "What do you believe about all this," waving his arm around to take in the valley, the village, the mountains and more. "How did this," he bent down and picked up a handful of dirt, let it trickle through his fingers, "come to be?"

White Knife nodded, grinning as he understood, "Ah, we believe in a creator that made all good things, and an evil spirit that made bad things." He pointed to the sun, "The sun, the earth, and the moon are gods that give to us, and there are many things that have powers, like the eagle," then nodding at Wolf, "wolf, bear, and more. We believe in these powers and many have a totem," he touched a small pouch at his waist, "with special things that have power."

Gabe nodded, then asked again, "But if you were killed that night at my place, then what?"

White Knife frowned, "Then I would be buried like we buried the others." He looked at Gabe, frowning and asked, "What is it that you believe about these things?"

Gabe grinned, continued walking beside White Knife and began to explain, "We believe in a Creator also. But the Creator we believe in, we call God. God created all things, the sun," nodding to the sky then gesturing to the ground, "the earth, the moon, and all things, including you and me. I believe that there is but one true God, and He is over all things, and there is no other god. He made me," then pinched his skin, "and you," and touched Knife's arm, "and my brother, Black Buffalo. We are all different, but He made us all. Not to kill each other, but to learn from each other and to live as he would have us live."

"What about when you die?"

Gabe grinned, "That's the best part! When we die, if we have put our faith in Him and Him alone, then we will have Heaven forever and we will live forever."

White Knife frowned, "I must learn more of this God of yours."

26 / CONSIDERATION

White Knife and Gabe spent the rest of the day learning and talking about the things most important to them both. After going into great detail about the things of God as told about in the Bible, even taking his own from the saddle bags and showing the words on page to White Knife, Gabe realized he had covered everything from creation to the life and death of Christ. White Knife was an eager learner and followed and understood most of what Gabe had said but he frowned as he considered, "Why would the Father God have his son die?"

Gabe dropped his eyes, thought a moment, opened the Bible and read John 3:16 *"For God so loved the world,* That's you and me and your people and my people. He loved the world and loves the world now. . ." He paused as he saw the furrows on White Knife's forehead deepen. Gabe waited.

Finally White Knife looked up, still frowning, and asked, "Loved?"

"You know, the way you feel about your wife and child. The way you feel about your mother and father and your people," explained Gabe, touching his fist to his chest to show the emotion.

"I feel that way about my mother and father because they are my mother and father. I feel that way about my wife because I bought her with six fine horses, and she gave me a son. But if this love you speak about would make one kill his own son, it is not a good thing!"

Gabe was surprised at White Knife's reaction and was speechless for a moment, but knew he had to explain. He looked at White Knife, "You have gone to battle with your enemies to protect your wife and son and your people. You do that because you love them and do not want them to die at the hand of your enemy. Is that right?"

"Yes, I do that."

"You are willing to die if it saves your family and your people from dying?"

"Yes, I would die to save them, but I would not have my son die for someone I did not know."

"Yet that is what Jesus did for us. The father God did not *make* him die, Jesus *chose* to die so we would not have to pay the price for our sin or the many times we have done wrong."

"But we still die?"

"Yes. But the penalty for sin is death and hell forever! But if we accept what Jesus did for us when He died in our place, when we die we will go to Heaven!"

White Knife frowned again, then remembered their earlier conversation, "Ah, yes. The place where everything is good and forever," nodding as he spoke. "So, because this Jesus died so we can go to Heaven?"

"Yes. That's the gift of God, eternal life, so we can live forever in Heaven."

White Knife dropped his gaze to the coals simmering in the cookfire before them, then looked up at Gabe, "I must think on this. It is much to consider." He smiled as he nodded, then looked to his wife, Little Rabbit, as she readied their meal, "Now, we will eat."

Gabe grinned, knowing their time of discussion was done and White Knife's attention was on the meal and other things. Gabe twisted around to get comfortable, rested his hand on Wolf's scruff and watched at Little Rabbit filled the trenchers with the hot stew. The sun was lowering toward the mountains behind them and Gabe was thinking about making the journey home by moonlight, he was anxious to see his family. He looked at White Knife, started to speak, but White Knife spoke first. "We will go to the lodge of my father, Old Owl. He wants you to come before the council and we will smoke the pipe."

Gabe cocked one eyebrow up as he looked at White

Knife, "Why does he want this?"

"You spoke of peace; the council must hear what you said for they are the ones that decide about peace. My father is known as the peace chief, my brother, Black Bear is the war leader of our people. The council of elders will listen to your words. If they agree, then the calumet will be passed for each one to offer their thoughts to the spirits."

Old Owl sat cross-legged, arms crossed on his chest showing the geometric dark tattoos on his upper arms and neck, his long braids hung over his shoulders, the beaver wrapping intertwined with the colored and braided sinew. His stoic expression seemed to set the tone for the group. To Old Owls' left sat Black Bear, war leader of the people, with long braids, scalp lock dangling to one side with a single feather, his broad shoulders marked with tattoos, his biceps showing thin silver bands, and his chest held the bone hair pipe breast plate with beaded and decorated spacings.

To the right of Old Owl was a stoic man, Wind Maker, the calumet lying across his legs, his hands resting on his knees, the buffalo cape and crown with horns showing him to be the Shaman of the people. He scowled at Gabe as he sat with White Knife across the fire amidst the other members of the council.

At Old Owl's direction, Gabe stood to tell of the fight with the raiders that sought to steal the horses and the deadly confrontation with Many Bears and his vengeance seekers. When he concluded, Old Owl motioned for him to be seated as he added to Gabe's remarks, "You know that Spirit Bear spared the life of my son when he could have easily taken it, and White Knife returned to tell of this man. What my son says is the same as what Spirit Bear spoke." Old Owl looked at the others around the circle, then added, "We know of Many Bears and that after this council had talked of peace, he led a war party against the Arapaho and lost one hand of our young warriors. His hunt for vengeance took him and more of our young warriors to go against Spirit Bear in revenge for the killing of his brother, but this man," nodding to Gabe, "warned Many Bears not to try for vengeance, but he did not listen, and more than one hand of our warriors did not return." The revered leader looked at each of the members of the council, "Now, this man seeks peace by coming into our village alone and in peace. He has not attacked, he has not stolen, but has done what any of us would do, fight for his family."

Old Owl breathed deep, glanced to Wind Maker and to the calumet on his lap, then to the council members, "We should smoke the pipe and make peace with this man and his people." No one moved or spoke as silence filled the hide lodge, until one man near the back of the group stood and shouted, "NO! This man killed my brother and many other warriors of our people! And you now seek peace?! He should be bound, beaten by the women, and hung above the fires to be burned for our dead warriors!" he was screaming and jumping as he spoke, "Are the great Comanche warriors or women! We should have vengeance, not peace!" As he pushed through the crowd to come closer to the council members, the light of the fire showed the man to be Many Bears, his arm still bound and splinted, but fire flared in his eyes and spittle flew as he screamed his war cry, arching his back, his face lifted to the peak of the lodge and thumped his chest with his good arm.

When Many Bears finished his rant and stood glaring at Old Owl and the others, the chief spoke in the same tone as he already had as he looked around the circle of elders. "Many Bears' grief and hunger for vengeance has clouded his mind. It has always been the custom of our people to treat anyone that comes to our camp in peace, to treat them with respect and treat them as a friend, giving food and shelter while they are with us. Yet Many Bears would have us break the very custom of our people and make this man our prisoner and torture him as a bitter enemy. Yet this man has made no attack on our people, has shown himself to be a man of honor and has only acted in defense of his family. He has proven himself to be a great warrior and seeks only to be a friend of the Comanche and live in peace with our people."

He paused again to let his words be considered, then added, "Many Bears chose to ignore the words of this council and go to war with the Arapaho, and then led our young warriors to their death when he ignored the warning of this man who sought to give them life. And after fighting one on one with Spirit Bear, and Spirit Bear sparing his life, Many Bears is shamed by his own actions and failures. Now he would have us ignore our own customs and our own council." He shook his head slowly, glared at the stubborn Many Bears who stood fuming before him, then turned to the others, "Let us smoke the pipe with Spirit Bear."

At those words, Many Bears screamed his war cry again and stormed from the lodge, slapping the entry blanket aside and kicking at anything that hindered his way. The others sat still for a moment, some shaking their heads in disgust at the outburst of Many Bears, but all showed their agreement with Old Owl's guidance by pounding their fists against the ground before them. When the sound gave way to silence, Old Owl accepted the lit pipe from Wind Maker, looked around the circle and lifted the pipe to the four directions, the heavens and the earth, and drew a deep draught, exhaled the smoke slowly, then passed the pipe to his right. As Gabe accepted the calumet, he admired the carved soapstone bowl that was the image of an eagle's claw, the long stem decorated with beadwork and quills, the fan of feathers that hung below, and the carved soapstone mouthpiece. He repeated the actions of the others and passed the pipe to his right.

When the circle was completed, Old Owl handed the pipe to Wind Maker who tapped out the dottle and sat the pipe aside. Old Owl spoke, "It has been spoken, the spirits have been honored, so let it be done." He nodded to the others and they slowly rose to leave. At Old Owl's motion, Gabe and White Knife remained after the others left. The chief looked at Gabe, a slight grin tugging at the corners of his mouth, and he spoke, "We are friends and at peace with one another. But Many Bears is an angry man and not to be trusted. White Knife said you are leaving soon, but you must be careful of Many Bears, he finds it easy to influence the young men that seek honors, and he could still come against you."

Gabe nodded, "I understand Old Owl. And I am honored that you have agreed to this peace between us. But I must tell you, if Many Bears tries anything again, I will show him no mercy. If others come with him, they should know what they face. The two fights have been against me and my woman, Cougar Woman. But if others come, they will face us and my friend, Black Buffalo, and his woman Grey Dove. Black Buffalo is known as a great warrior, but he is not known for his mercy. If they come, many will die."

White Knife spoke up, "I will let them know the

wishes of the council. Perhaps they will choose to follow others in peace or on hunts and not follow Many Bears."

Old Owl nodded, then looked at Gabe, "My son has said you gave him the drink of coffee, but you had little. You should know, our scouts have told of the coming of some comancheros, traders from the south that bring goods of the people of Mexico. They will be here tomorrow. Perhaps they will have this coffee and more."

Gabe grinned, "I was thinking about leaving tonight, but if the traders have coffee, it would be good to stay until they come."

Old Owl nodded, grinning, and Gabe and White Knife rose to leave. White Knife said, "I will find those that would follow Many Bears and speak to them. They are young and anxious for battle and honors; they must make their own choices."

"I understand, but death is not a good choice," cautioned Gabe as he started to his lodge for the night.

27 / COMANCHEROS

"So, tell me about these Comancheros, the traders your father spoke about. You mentioned them before, but I know little of them." stated Gabe, as he accepted the fry bread from Little Rabbit. The two men sat across from one another, the low cookfire popping and snarling with new flame as the woman pushed another stick into the coals. It was just after first light, the billowy clouds with pink tinted bellies beneath the dark puffy heads of the big clouds hung like a curtain over the wide band of blue and pink that heralded the new day. At White Knife's invitation, Gabe had joined his family before their lodge while the village began to stir with the anticipation of the coming of traders.

White Knife looked at Gabe, leaned back against his willow back rest and began. "My father's father told of trading with the Spanish of the pueblos along the river known as the Rio Grande. The people would meet at the pueblos for a gathering of traders and bands of the people. The Spanish called them *Asuntos de negocios.* They would bring their burros and *carretas* with beads, cloth, tobacco, coffee, sugar, kettles, blankets, knives and more. Our people would trade horses, hides, pelts, dried meat, and captives." He paused, chuckling, "My grandfather would tell of the times when he and others would raid the villages and pueblos, steal the horses and captives, then sell them back to the traders." He laughed, looked up at Gabe, "His favorite story was about one of the captives, a woman, who was taken and traded back many times. He said she would run out with her hands up when he and the other raiders came and would climb up on any warrior's horse. She said she wanted to get away from her husband!" he laughed as he remembered the story. "But the warrior would be glad to trade her back because she was like a magpie, always talking and doing nothing! It was after this time that our people had a great battle with the Spanish and our people, led by *Cuerno Verde,* Green Horn, and we were defeated."

"In my father's time, when I was but a small boy, our people agreed to a peace with the Spanish." He paused, stirred the coals, and looked up at Gabe, "One of our war leaders, Ecueracapa, led our people to sign with the Spanish and have peace and the traders began to come to our villages. That was the first time I had pinole. My mother used it to bake bread and it was good!"

Gabe grinned, nodding, "I have had pinole in a hot drink, it is good. But I like coffee better!"

A ruckus at the lower end of the camp told of the arrival of the traders. Men came from their lodges, lifted bundles with hides and pelts to their shoulders and started after their women who were hustling youngsters, bearing cradle boards on their backs, and carrying their own bundles of goods to trade. The people chattered among themselves, giddy with the excitement of the long-awaited traders and the goods they would have to offer. The traders usually came in the season of colors, but this visit was a welcome interlude in the unusually dry summer.

The men rose, White Knife snatching up a prepared bundle beside the lodge and Little Rabbit already starting toward the gathering and started to the lower end of the camp where the traders would set up shop. Most of the village had gathered, a wide semi-circle watching as the traders with their *carretas,* loaded to overflowing, began arranging their goods on the many fanned out blankets that lay before the wagons. It was a wide assortment with one grouping showing kettles, pots, butcher knives, and similar items. Another group had bolts of calico, wool, and stacks of blankets, bundles of hard baked cornbread, and bags of pinole and coffee. The third group had an

abundance of beads, needles, mirrors, knives, hatch-
ets, vermillion, and verdigris.

Four men were busy with the goods, one man
was the obvious leader, barking orders and directing the displays. He was a big man, barrel chested,
no neck, mutton chop whiskers and long scraggly
and greasy hair. Puffed lips that did little to hide his
tobacco-stained teeth, a leather vest strained to cover
the pompous paunch, canvas britches were bloused
over laced boots. Gabe thought the man was a strange
mix of French Coeur de Bois, and Spanish Grena-
dier, acting like a soldier in command of recalcitrant
troops, but overseeing the trades like a Coeur de
Bois. In short order, they were ready for trades and
the crowd pushed forward and the bartering began.
Gabe walked casually among the people, watching the
activity, until he spotted what appeared to be bags of
coffee, then he pushed closer.

The trader, a man of middle age, a touch of grey
showing in his wavy black hair, a hint of amusement
in his eyes, spoke confidently in the tongue of the
people as he dickered over the trade. He glanced up
when Gabe came near and surprise showed on his
face as he frowned, and stated in Spanish, "You are
not Comanche!"

Gabe chuckled, "Nope. But, if you've got coffee, I
sure could use some!"

The man extended his hand, "I am Alvero Vasquez,

pleased to meet you," he lifted his eyebrows in question, waiting for Gabe to give his name.

Gabe grinned, reached to shake the man's hand and answered, "I am known as Spirit Bear, or Gabe."

Alvero grinned, "We have coffee. How much would you like?"

"That depends on what you are asking for it!" answered Gabe, ever the cautious one.

"Ahh, a shrewd trader. Well, what do you have to trade?"

"I've a few gold coins, American."

The man's eyebrows lifted, and he grinned, "Gold! We don't see that very often," exclaimed Alvero, giving a quick glance to the bigger man who Gabe had counted as the leader. The glance resulted in the big man slowly making his way near, and Alvero introduced him, "Gabe, this is our captain, Manolo Guerrero. Captain, this is Gabe, or Spirit Bear."

The big man forced a grin to part his chops, showing his grungy teeth, as he nodded and extended his meaty paw to shake. Gabe accepted the offer and shook hands, surprised at the softness of the man's palms and realized he did little work, but ordered the others to the tasks. The man's eyes flashed with as much greed as his clothes showed in grime. The odor of long unwashed body was almost overpowering, and Gabe stepped back a little, pretending to look around the trader at some of the goods. He heard

Alvero speak softly to the big man, "He wants coffee and wants to pay in gold."

The big man nodded and turned toward Gabe, "So, you need some coffee?"

"Oh, I wouldn't say need, but I would like to get some, if you have it," answered Gabe, feeling the edge of the trade blanket. He glanced up to the big man, "Do you? Have any, I mean?"

"Yes, yes. And we have pinole also. Have you enjoyed the hot drink of pinole?"

"Yes, I have. I might take some of that also," he replied, watching the big man as he gestured to Alvero to get the goods.

When Alvero returned, he carried a large rough linen bag, and a slightly smaller bag, the size of a haversack. He sat them down at the edge of the blanket, pulled a pair of small pouches from his waist band and looked to Gabe, "And how much would you like, sir?"

Gabe grinned, "That depends on what you think its worth?" glancing from Alvero to Manolo. The big man nodded to Alvero, looked to Gabe, "By the pound, one dollar American!" he stated, grinning. "As you know, coffee is expensive, even in port when it comes off the ships!"

Gabe looked at the bags, guessed the bigger one to hold about twenty-five pounds of coffee, the smaller one about fifteen pounds of pinole. He looked at Manolo, "I'm not one to spend all day dickering. I will," and he reached into his tunic pocket and extracted two coins, held them up between his thumb and forefinger so Manolo could see the Liberty Cap image on one side and the Small Eagle on the other, "give you these two ten-dollar gold pieces for both bags," nodding to the two bags at the edge of the blanket.

Manolo's eyes gleamed with greed, as he looked from the coins to the bags, and back to Gabe, "If you have one more of those coins, we have a deal."

Gabe grinned, shook his head and breathed deep as he shrugged. "That's all the coin I have, but," he smiled as he thought and reached for a small pouch that hung from his belt, inside his britches. He brought it out, opened it by spreading the draw cords, and dug around inside, then extracted a small gold nugget. He had watched the reaction of the big man who leaned forward to look while Gabe dug in the bag. He held up the small nugget, "I'll give you this instead of the coins!"

Manolo frowned, "You got more of those in there?"

"No, no," replied Gabe, digging in the bag to extract a piece of turquoise, "just some blue rock for my woman." He held it out in his palm for the men to see, then put it back in the pouch. Manolo put his hand to his mouth, frowning as he thought, "The nugget and one of the coins!"

Gabe nodded, "Agreed!" and extended his hand to

shake and seal the deal.

Gabe handed over the nugget and coin, bent down and picked up the two bags and turned to start back to the upper end of the village. As he left, Manolo looked at Alvero and growled, "He has more, and I mean to get it!"

He turned away from Alvero and almost knocked down a man that stood close behind him. Manolo growled, pushing at the man, "Git outta my way!" he bellered in Comanche. But the man he pushed, one arm bound in a splint, countered with, "He does have more!" looking around to watch Gabe disappear among the lodges.

"What do you mean?" snarled Manolo.

"He has more of those," hissed Many Bears, pointing to Manolo's hand that gripped the gold. "I saw him take that from his bags at his saddle. He has much more."

"Do you know where he stays? Or where he's goin'?" asked Manolo, glaring at the Comanche.

Many Bears nodded. "I know where he is, where he is going, and where he lives!"

"Why are you tellin' me this?" asked Manolo, showing his usual skeptical manner.

"I want him dead! He killed my brother!"

Manolo grinned, "Let's talk."

28 / RUSE

White Knife watched as Gabe finished loading the grey packhorse, preparing to leave. Gabe suggested, "Since you know where we live, maybe you and Little Rabbit could come for a visit. It would be good for our women to meet each other."

White Knife grinned and nodded, "Maybe your woman could teach Little Rabbit about wounds and such," touching his shoulder that had healed well after Cougar Woman's initial bandaging. He grew somber, dropping his eyes to the ground, looked back at Gabe as he swung aboard the big black. "Many Bears was talking with the Comancheros after you traded for the coffee. They were talking about you and watched you walk away with the bags."

Gabe settled into the saddle, looked down at White Knife, "You think they're up to something?"

White Knife nodded, "I will watch them, but Many

Bears is still angry and wants vengeance. The council spoke against him, but he will try again."

Gabe nodded, picked up the rein at Ebony's withers, breathed a heavy sigh and answered White Knife, "I will also watch for them, but I will show no mercy. If there are young warriors with him, you should warn them."

White Knife nodded, reached up to Gabe and the men clasped forearms, "You are a friend," declared White Knife and stepped back.

The sun was high and the shadows almost non-existent as Gabe rode from the camp of the Comanche. Several of the villagers waved as he passed, a few boys chased after Wolf who ignored them, and the edge of the line of lodges was soon behind them. He pushed toward the river, determined to take the same trail on his return. A casual glance to the diminished crowd near the traders showed a couple of the comancheros were packing up a pair of wagons, but another man was busy with the last of the trades. There was no sign of the ramrod, the sizable man would be hard to miss if he were present.

There was no distinct trail from the camp to the river, most hunters and others always choosing a different way to and from as to not leave a worn trail that would become too traveled and obvious. He wound through the sage, greasewood, and rabbit brush, passing the large clumps of prickly pear cactus and the occasional cluster of cholla, most of it blooming bright pink. The crashing of the rapids cascading over the rocks beckoned from beyond the cottonwoods and Gabe leaned back in the saddle as Ebony gingerly stepped down the rocky bank. The big black stepped into the water, the grey coming alongside, and both dipped their noses in the cold, clear water and took a deep drink, until Wolf splashed in upstream and muddied the water as he paddled across the low rapids that chuckled over the smaller donies.

Gabe dug his heels in to move Ebony across the gravelly bottom and make his way across shallow waters. Gabe looked upstream, glanced at the high-water marks on the banks, and guessed the spring runoff was over and the drought was already taking its toll. Ebony stretched out and hunched up as he climbed the bank, stopped on the dry ground, and shook, rattling everything that wasn't tied down, then stepped out as if nothing happened. Gabe shook his head, chuckling, watched Wolf roll his hide, shake, and finally roll in the grass to rid himself of the river water, then glanced to the Grey who had also shook and stepped out behind the black.

The first couple miles into the narrow valley of the Arkansa river, the slopes on Gabe's right were gradual and sparsely covered with piñon and spruce, buffalo grass and rabbit brush. The trail held to the high bank and hugged the hillsides and slopes. Across the river, the hills flanked the river, often ending in sheer precipices into the water. When the river made a series of snake like bends back upon itself, the trail sided the hills and let the river take its course nearer the south side rocky hills. Soon the valley opened and pushed the hills back, leaving a flat-bottomed valley that showed bunch grass and sage, but little else. At its widest, the valley was no more than a half mile, until it was folded into the foothills just past a dog-leg bend of the river.

The river had carved its way through the steep sided hills that now flanked the waterway, pushing it from one side to the other, almost like a dance of rocks and hills. Another three miles and the mouth of the narrow valley of the river opened to show the broad valley that lay before them. The majestic Sawatch range of mountains stood on the west edge like a garrison of giants, mustered in a long line, shoulder to shoulder, and watching over the fertile valley as if it were the stage of eternity where life and death were the players and all of nature the cheering crowd.

He had been thinking of Cougar Woman and the boys, Ezra, and his family, and was anxious to be home, but thoughts of Many Bears and the Comancheros kept crowding in and he knew he could not lead these renegades to his home and family. If they were on his trail, he would pick both the time and place of their confrontation, and it would be nowhere near the cabin.

He glanced up at the sun, guessed it to be late afternoon, pushing toward dusk, and although he could make it home, it would be well after dark, and that would not work with the plan forming in his mind. He breathed deep, feeling that familiar crawling up his spine and neck, and he knew he was being followed. How many and where, he did not know, but that mattered little. He stood in his stirrups, surveyed the terrain before him, and nodded as he spotted a shoulder that would be far enough into the valley to afford him choices, and he dropped into his saddle, waved Wolf ahead and nudged Ebony to follow.

He reined up at a clump of juniper, stepped down and left a trail to the river and back, walked around a little and carefully went to the rocks, and climbed atop a high ridge that would afford a view of his back trail and hopefully the canyon of the river. Wolf padded beside him, and they mounted the ridge, crossed a narrow gulch, and climbed to a higher point. A quick glance showed the silvery ribbon of the river winding through the narrow canyon, and he dropped to the ground, took his seat with knees raised to support his elbows and stretched out the brass telescope. He searched every piece of the trail he could see, watching for any movement or dust, but saw nothing. He lifted the scope to look to the wide flat just beyond the dog-leg bend of the river and slowly scanned the entire flat. He saw nothing, lowered the scope, and looked at Wolf, "I don't get it boy, I had that creepy crawling up my spine that I get when I know somethin' wrong or somethin's following us and I don't see anything."

Wolf cocked his head to the side, looked down the canyon and whimpered as he turned back to Gabe. "What is it boy? You see somethin'?"

Gabe stretched out the scope again, made a quick survey of the near end of the trail, followed it through the canyon, then lifted the scope to scan the flats once again. There! Coming into the flats from the far end, riders, three, no four. Gabe grinned as he followed their movements and even though they were far away, it was obvious that one of them was of considerable size and Gabe guessed him to be the big Comanchero, Manolo Guerrero.

Gabe lowered the scope, looked down at Wolf, grinning, "Thanks boy, I almost missed 'em! Let's get back to the horses and see if we can set up a welcome for our visitors!" Gabe slid back from the crest, rolled over and came to his feet and retraced his steps to the horses. With a thorough scan of the area for any obvious sign, Gabe was satisfied with his leavings and stepped aboard Ebony and started on the trail, moving upstream with the river.

He knew the others were no more than an hour, at

most two, behind him and he would have to choose his site and lay the trap before they came near. The river bent back to the north to follow the long line of foothills on the east side of the valley, the smaller fork that came from the western mountains chuckled over the rocks and joined the main stream, but Gabe rode to the north. He could not make camp too soon, it would appear suspicious if he stopped before dusk, and he pushed on another couple miles. The sun was cradled between the tall peaks to the west when Gabe saw the tall anthill shaped bald hill on his right and heard the chuckling of the river as it cascaded over the rocks to his left. He rode closer to the water, saw a possible crossing over the gravel bottomed shallows, looked at the far shore and a sizable thicket of mature cottonwoods framed a grassy knoll that would fit his needs.

In a short while, Gabe had the camp set up, a fire going, the horses stripped and tethered on the back side of the knoll where there was ample grass for graze, and his bedroll rolled out at the edge of the circle of light from the fire. He sat down on the log and slipped the Mongol bow from the case and started stringing his favorite weapon. As he worked, he pictured the lay of the land, the trees, river, rocks and more that would offer cover both to him and his attackers and calculated his moves and their possible reactions. He had hidden his rifle and saddle pistols in the trees, buried the saddle bags with the gold in the bottoms in the brush and leaves, and lay the panniers, packs, and saddles in sight at the edge of the light. With the bow strung, he hung the quiver of arrows at his belt, looked over the camp and with Wolf at his side, silently slipped into the trees.

29 / AMBUSH

"If we go with you against this man, what is there for us?" asked Snake Eater, one of several young warriors that had come to Many Bears lodge when they heard about a war party.

"This one man killed our brothers! We must take vengeance upon him!" snarled Many Bears, his anger spewing with his words. But he saw the reaction of the others and knew they were not concerned with vengeance, only honors and booty. He looked from one to the other, "Did you not see the fine horses this man has? And there are more at his lodge with his woman! He has the white man's weapons, those that are held with one hand, and the bigger one called a rifle."

The young warriors grinned, nudged one another, and laughed, anticipating the coming fight and the honors they would gain. One of their number, a somber man known as Head in the Clouds, spoke up, "Did not Old Owl and White Knife warn us of following you? The others that went with you did not return! Why should we go?"

"They are women!" spat Many Bears. "If you come, you will gain many honors, horses, maybe women and more! If you stay in the village, what honor will you have?"

"What does this man want with the white man?" asked Snake Eater, pointing to the Comanchero with his chin.

"This man wants the yellow rock the white man carries! And like me, he wants the white man dead because of the way he talked to him!"

Manolo Guerrero, the leader of the Comanchero, stepped forward and growled, "If you are a warrior, then you will come with us! This man has enough bounty to make all of you honored by your people. You will have enough horses to trade for a woman! You will have the weapons of the white man that will make you great warriors! You will show the others," he spat as he spoke, "you are the real warriors of your village!"

"Why do you want the white man's yellow rocks?"

Manolo huffed, shook his head, "I can take that yellow rock back to Santa Fe and buy rifles and other weapons, bring them back here so you will have the power of the white man!"

"Aiiieeee," shouted Snake Eater. "I go! Who will come with us?" He looked around at the small group of young warriors, but most, probably influenced more by Old Owl and White Knife, turned away to leave. Only one remained, a close friend to Snake Eater that followed him wherever, Water Horse. He looked to Snake Eater, nodded, and stepped closer.

The two men looked at Many Bears and Manolo, and heard Many Bears grumble, "He is only one man! We will be enough!" He glared at the two young warriors, "You can have his horses, I will take his weapons!" Snake Eater and Water Horse looked at one another, nodding as they grinned at the thought of the fine horses of the white man, and what honors they would have when they rode back into the village upon those horses.

Many Bears looked at the two, "Get your horses and weapons, we leave soon!"

Manolo and Many Bears stood behind the lodge of Many Bears and watched Gabe as he rode from the village, they had agreed they would follow him and take him and his goods when he was far from the village and their deed would not be known by the people of the Comanche. Many Bears knew he would be shamed and shunned if he went against the will of the council after Old Owl had agreed to peace with the white man, but if they did not know, then Many

Bears would have his vengeance and the bounty of the white man. Blinded by his vengeance, he gave no thought that when he returned with the weapons or horses of the white man, his people would know that he had done wrong, but like so many evildoers, he was unconcerned with the consequences, because he believed no one would know.

Manolo looked down at Many Bears, "If we take the others with us, they will know what was done and will tell others. Then you will have to face the council!"

Many Bears shook his head, "They will be useful, perhaps as a distraction or more, but if they do not return to the village, they can tell no one!"

Manolo slowly nodded, letting a grin split his hoary countenance, as a chuckle escaped his lips. "Then I reckon we oughta be for gettin' ready. Don't want him gettin' too fer ahead of us!"

"I know the trail he takes, he cannot get away," mumbled Many Bears.

It was a short while before the two young warriors returned, excitement showing on their faces and in their eyes. Both had quivers across their backs, a bow lay across the withers of their horses, a tomahawk and knife in their belts and a bedroll behind them. The horses had a simple surcingle over a blanket, crude stirrups attached, with a simple rein that encircled their lower jaws to give the riders control.

Although the men were not painted for war, the horses had some paint to give extra strength and power in battle; a hand print on the hip, lightning bolts down the forelegs, spots on the rumps, and more, all with the purpose of giving the riders an edge over their enemies.

Snake Eater spoke, "We saw the white man leave."

"And we will follow, but not so close as to be seen!" answered Many Bears.

They soon took to the trail, the tracks of the white man and his pack horse easily visible and followed. "He has no reason to think anyone is following," declared Many Bears as he motioned to the tracks. "He has not stopped, or turned to look back, he is a fool! We can be upon him before he knows we are near!"

"I'm thinkin' it best to wait until he camps for the night, then hit him. You said he was a crafty one, settin' traps an' all. Don't need to take any chances we don't have to, so if'n he don't know we're followin' he won't set no traps!" answered the big man.

Many Bears grunted his response, then nudged his mount ahead to examine the tracks as he leaned down then sat erect to look up the trail. He nodded and glanced to the sun to consider the remaining daylight. He looked back at Manolo, "We will be in the valley before dark. It is open, little cover, we could be seen."

"Then we'll just need to hang back a mite, won't we?"

It was dusk when the tracks of the white man showed he had dismounted and led the horses to water. Many Bears also stepped down to examine the sign, seeing nothing to indicate anything other than a brief rest stop. Although the moccasin prints showed the white man had walked about, it appeared as nothing but him stretching his legs and relieving himself. Many Bears swung back aboard and signaled the others to follow.

The sun had dropped behind the western mountains and dusk had lost its glow when the renegades sided the river, staying on the trail of their prey. With the dim moonlight, the tracks of the white man's horses were still easily seen, each footfall of the horses breaking the soil to show the moist dirt underneath. The hoofprints appearing as a dark mark on the dusty soil that held little more than cholla and prickly pear with random clumps of bunch grass.

Dusk had just dropped the curtain of darkness that lay like a heavy blanket across the valley bottom. The eastern hills stood in deep shadows as the moon was waning from full and scattered clouds masked the stars, yet there was ample light for Gabe to see what was coming. The bank on the east side of the river was no more than five or six feet above water level and sloped gently to the sand bar at water's edge. The west bank where Gabe waited, was about ten or twelve feet above the river, and rose steeply to the flat, so much so, that the trail from the river angled across its grassy face. The slight bend of the river had captured a pile of storm water debris, logs, limbs, rocks and more that were piled high from some past high-water flood. The big cottonwood log that stood askew atop the debris offered Gabe a view of the far bank and cover in the shadows.

Gabe watched the flats beyond the greenery at river's edge, waiting for any indication of the renegades. His view of the far side was limited, and he glanced over his shoulder at a towering cottonwood and back to the distant shore. He looked at Wolf, "I think I'll shinny up that tree yonder and have a look see to the other side, you keep watch from here." He chuckled as he stepped closer to the big tree, slipped the bow over his head and shoulder, and with handholds in the deep grooved bark, he worked his way up to the first big branch that would give him a better view. Within moments he was at his selected perch and turned to look across the river.

The scattered clouds cast long shadows, but the patchwork quilt of moonlight afforded Gabe a short glance at the four riders that kept close to the trees and greenery that lined the bank of the river. They rode two by two with the big man on the near side of the leading pair. Gabe shook his head, knowing there were two things that almost all evildoers have in common; they think they are smarter than everyone else, and their greed makes them lazy, too lazy to work for what they want and choosing to take it from others by whatever means necessary. And that laziness usually dulled whatever intelligence they may have which usually leads to their downfall. Gabe watched as the four reined up, and saw the big man apparently giving the others orders as he gestured about, motioning both up and down the river. Gabe guessed they had seen the light from his low burning campfire, and they were now formulating their plan to attack.

Having seen all he needed; Gabe slipped down the back side of the cottonwood to return to his promontory atop the storm driftwood. Had he stayed aloft a bit longer, he might have seen the distant figures of more riders, but his eagerness for the confrontation bid him to lower ground. From here, he had a good view of the crossing and the clearing of his camp, with a clear field of fire to both. He saw one of the Comanche had gone to foot and was moving upstream of the crossing. Gabe grinned as he thought, *Reckon one'll go up to come around behind me, the other'n'll go downstream to come from down thataway. That means Many Bears and the big guy'll come straight on across. Alright fellas, if that's what you want, come ahead on!*

30 / STRIKE

Gabe motioned Wolf to go, "Get the one below the horses!" he whispered, sending the big black away. Wolf padded off into the darkness, becoming one with the night shadows. Gabe gave a quick look across the river to see if the Comanchero and Many Bears had started their movement, but seeing nothing, he turned into the trees above the clearing. He could move through the woods as silently as the night breeze, disturbing nothing, seen by no one. Moving slowly in the shadows, he was reassured by the distant call of a poorwill that sounded his two-tone call to his neighbors. Above him, a great horned owl asked for Gabe's identity to let him pass, but the nighthawk's shrill peent came from higher in the tree. Gabe grinned, seeking to pierce the darkness with his stare, searching the narrow shafts of moonlight for the warrior sent by the

Comanchero to come from upstream.

Gabe slowly lifted one foot, paused as he watched the trees and shrubs, moved it forward and lowered it into the grass, feeling every blade with his toes and exposed ankles. He shifted his weight, avoiding the nearby rough barked cottonwood, knowing even the brushing of his buckskin across the bark would sound like the dragging of a rough log across gravel. Another step, pause, look, and wait, move again, letting his form blend with the twisted trees and saplings. He saw movement, the impatient young warrior was moving quietly, but he moved too fast, too soon, and Gabe centered his attention on the man, yet kept his eyes to the side for there is something in a man that senses when he is watched, but only when the eyes of another are locked on his image.

With slow breaths that lifted his chest but little, the only movement from Gabe, he waited as the warrior moved closer to the campsite. The nearer he came to the glow of the fire, the more his attention would be focused on the camp and he would be unaware of danger from behind. Gabe saw the man go to a slight crouch as he brought his bow with nocked arrow before him. Gabe grinned, and moved behind the man, slowly slipping his pistol from his belt. With the barrel gripped tightly, Gabe raised the pistol slowly, and quickly brought the butt of the grip down on the side of the man's head, stealing consciousness from him as he started to slump to the ground. Gabe caught him before he crumpled and slowly lowered him quietly to the ground.

Gabe snatched a length of rawhide from his belt, bound the man's hands behind him and around a sapling as he pulled him up and back against the cold bark. He slipped the man's moccasin off his foot and stuffed it in his mouth, then stepped back to examine his handiwork. He picked up the man's bow, lifted his tomahawk and knife from his belt, grabbed a handful of arrows from the quiver and stacked the bunch under some willows out of sight of the warrior. Satisfied, he retrieved the Mongol bow and started back to the clearing.

Wolf padded quietly past the tethered horses, his scent familiar to the animals and caused no alarm. He moved into the trees, following the scent he recognized as Comanche. His lithe body moved through the brush and saplings, soft fur making not a sound as he rubbed against the small branches. His eyes flared orange as he watched the shadows for movement, detecting the presence of the man coming near. He lowered himself to his belly, watching and waiting. As the man came near, he was moving in a slight crouch, a bow with a nocked arrow held before him.

Wolf watched and slowly rose, his head lowered below his shoulders as he moved quieter than the shadows about him, approaching the man from the side that held the arrow. One long stride, another, another, then he shifted his weight to his hind legs and sprung forward, his black form flying through the night as a moving shadow, melting into the darkness. His one hundred seventy-five pounds concentrated on his forepaws as he struck the man against his shoulder, stretching his head forward, mouth open, teeth bared. He rode the startled man to the ground, his teeth buried in the man's throat, stifling any cry until they struck the ground. The bow shattered; the man struggled to cry out, but the sound was lost in the gurgle of blood.

He kicked and thrashed but Wolf's teeth bore deeper until he snarled and swung his head side to side to tear out the meat of the man's throat, blood flying and splattering on the grass and nearby shrubs. Another kick and the man lay still, Wolf astraddle of his body, as the big beast, breathing heavily, glared down at the bloodied face of the man. Wolf pushed against the man's face with his muzzle, lifted his eyes to the trees toward the clearing, then stepped off the body and started back to the clearing, keeping to the shadows.

As Gabe neared the camp, the shadows danced in the flickering light of the low burning campfire, but nothing moved in the clearing. He watched, moving side to side, staying back, and keeping his eyes averted from the fire so as not to ruin his night vision, and waited but a moment. He slipped back to his perch atop the driftwood pile and searched the far bank for any sign of the big man and Many Bears. The clatter of hooves against stone brought his attention closer as he spotted two riders approaching the crossing. He frowned, surprised that they would make such a direct approach and on horseback, there was no stealth to a ridden horse.

Yet the men were making no pretense of stealth, Manolo riding in the lead, as they splashed across the gravelly bottomed river. When they struck the narrow sandbar at the edge of the bank, the Comanchero nudged his horse to the trail that angled across the face of the bank and moved up the trail toward Gabe's camp, Many Bears came close behind. As they approached the crest, the big man called out, "Hellooo the camp! Hellooo the camp! We're friendly! Can we come in?"

When no answer came, Manolo turned to Many Bears, "He's prob'ly in the trees, got us covered until he sees who we are, you hang back an' I'll ride in an' talk."

Gabe was close enough to hear the hushed tones of the conversation between the two and grinned at the subterfuge of the big man. He was certain both the Comanchero and Many Bears were expecting the two warriors to come against the camp and overwhelm him, but they were indisposed at the present time.

Gabe watched as the big man gigged his horse the rest of the way to crest the bank and ride into the light of the fire. As Manolo neared, he called out again, "We're friendly, just want a cup o' that coffee we're smellin'!"

Gabe shook his head at the man's gall, for there was no coffee on the fire. The campfire had burned low, small flames licking at the stubby ends of the firewood, a few embers climbing the thin pillar of smoke to add their glimmer to the night sky. Gabe watched Many Bears slip from his mount and move through the grass, intent on approaching the camp unseen and hopefully catching Gabe by surprise.

When Manolo saw the camp was empty, he lifted his voice and called out again, "Hey there stranger! We're in your camp and lookin' for you! You comin' out?"

Silence answered the big man as he sat silent and still aboard his sturdy mount, a broad chested bay gelding. The horse slowly lowered his head, smelling something he didn't like, probably the wolf who lay in the shadows at the edge of the camp, watching. The horse lifted his head, ears forward and began fidgeting as he stared into the darkness. The big man pulled the reins taut, reached down to stroke the neck of the bay, and spoke softly to him, reassuring him. But he looked around, searching the darkness, beginning to feel a little wary and nervous himself. He spoke softly to Many Bears, "He ain't nearby, but he cain't be fer, he wouldn't leave his horses."

Many Bears stepped from the trees, "Maybe Snake Eater got him, or Water Horse." He came into the circle of light, looking up at the big man, when he heard the voice from the darkness.

"Nope! I'm right here!" declared Gabe and quickly and silently moved away and behind the thicker trees. He knew he could not be seen, but arrows sent into the darkness after a sound are just as deadly as a well-aimed one. "Step down, make yourself comfortable!" he declared, quickly moving again yet watching the two men. He saw Many Bears holding a tomahawk at his side, one arm still splinted and bandaged. As Manolo swung a leg over the rump of his horse, Gabe caught a glimpse of a belt pistol and a tomahawk that had been hidden under the skirt of his jacket. Gabe touched the butt of the saddle pistol that sat in his sash. He had swapped the over/under Bailes belt pistol in favor of the large and more cumbersome saddle pistol. The saddle pistol was also an over under, but it had two locks and both barrels could be fired at the same time, or separately. While the Bailes had to have the barrels revolved and the hammer cocked again, the French saddle pistols were more easily managed.

"Well, we're down! You comin' into the light?" shouted Manolo, looking around. He lowered his voice and spoke softly to Many Bears, "You step to the side there, keep that hawk outta sight. I'll take him on, he won't expect that!"

Gabe heard the man speak, but was unable to understand what was said, but he did not need to hear the words to understand the intent. He knew they had no good intentions and could not be trusted. He lay the bow aside, dropped the quiver of arrows, and slipped the pistol from his sash. With the pistol held slightly behind him, Gabe stepped forward, letting a grin paint his face as he said, "So, to what do I owe this unexpected visit?" He spoke in the tongue of the Shoshoni, knowing Many Bears understood, and believing the big man would also. He glanced from one to the other, saw Many Bears start to side step a little, showing himself from behind the big man.

"We thought you might wanna do a little more tradin', I need me some more horses an' I understand you have some!" stated Manolo, trying to show a friendly face, and failing.

Gabe looked to Many Bears, "You! Stand still. You move again and you'll die!"

"Now, that's no way to talk!" declared the big man, then lifted his voice, "NOW!! Kill him!!"

Gabe was not surprised like Manolo expected, but grinned. "And who might you be talking to?" Gabe looked from Manolo to Many Bears, and spoke to the Comanche, "I told you to stand still!" pointing at him with his left hand, keeping the pistol obscured behind him.

Many Bears screamed and brought the tomahawk

back to throw, but the roar of the pistol as it spat smoke and lead startled him, causing a slight hesitation, but the impact of the big slug drove him back as it blossomed red on his chest, shattering his hair pipe breast plate. He staggered two steps, fell backwards, and landed in a crumpled heap. A moan escaped as he kicked and lay still.

At the time of Many Bears' scream, Manolo grabbed for his pistol, fumbling with the folds of his jacket and his pompous belly. He extracted the weapon, bringing it to full cock as he pulled, but stared at the muzzle of Gabe's pistol as he turned. The big man laughed, "You done fired that pistol, boy! Now, get ready to die!" as he started to lift his pistol. But the blast from the second barrel of Gabe's pistol stopped him, the slug smashed into his breast bone and drove it deep into the big man's chest. He grunted, looked down at the spurting blood and lifted his eyes to Gabe as he tottered side to side, his eyes unfocused. "You done kilt me! With a empty pistol!" he muttered as he leaned forward, stumbled, and tried to lift his head again.

The last thing he heard was the voice of Gabe as he said, "Two barrels. You shoulda counted 'em."

Gabe stepped back as the big man fell forward, rigid as a board, and bounced when he hit the ground, his face buried in the grass. Gabe stood still, looked from Manolo to Many Bears, and felt Wolf brush up against his leg. He looked down at his friend, who twisted his head up to look at Gabe, saw the blood on his jowls, then ran his fingers through his scruff, "Looks like you done your job, boy. Good boy!"

A slight rustle in the trees made Gabe drop to a knee as he twisted to face the new threat. His first thought was the bound warrior had freed himself and now was on the attack, but a familiar figure stepped from the darkness, and Gabe breathed easy. "White Knife! What brings you so far from your village?"

Gabe's Comanche friend stepped closer, followed by another familiar figure, "And you too, Black Bear? Welcome to my camp, although it's a little messy," nodding to the two bodies.

White Knife knew at a glance it was Many Bears and the Comanchero, and looked to Gabe, "The others?"

"I'm afraid one is dead. Wolf here did him in, back in the trees thataway. The other one is tied up and muffled back there," pointing to the trees upstream of the camp. "He's probably got a knot on his head, but he's alive."

Three other warriors had come from the trees into the light of the fire, and White Knife motioned for two to go find the bound man. He looked down at the body of Many Bears, back up at Gabe, "We will take the bodies of our dead. That one," motioning to the big man, "can lie where he lays."

"I'm sorry I had to do what I did, but they didn't leave me much choice. You could give his horse," nodding to the Comanchero, "and such, to the widows of the two, if you like. Hopefully with him gone," pointing to Many Bears with his chin, "I won't be getting anymore young bucks after my scalp."

"They have shamed our people. Old Owl and our people will understand if you no longer want to be at peace with our people."

Gabe shook his head, "White Knife, all I ever wanted was peace. Perhaps now, we can have that peace." He extended his arm and the two friends clasped forearms and touched each other's shoulder with their free hand. "And the invitation for you and Little Rabbit to visit still stands!"

Gabe watched as the band of Comanche crossed the river, the moonlight showing the way to the trail. He breathed deep and turned back to the horses. While the Comanche packed up their dead, Gabe had saddled Ebony and the grey packhorse. He knew sleep would be elusive and with the bright moonlight that appeared to be chasing the few clouds from the sky, he started for home. Looking to the stars, he located the Great Bear, or Ursa Major, then followed the line to locate the north star at the tip of the Lesser Bear. With the stars as his guide, he calculated it to be just after midnight and set the north star before him, angled a little to the left, and nudged Ebony to a ground eating canter. Wolf bounded alongside, tongue lolling as he often looked back to Gabe and the grey. With the camp behind them, and the fertile valley before them, they made good time. With an additional two miles behind, Gabe slowed the big black to a walk, giving him and the free reining grey a much-needed breather, but the stretching of the legs felt good to them all, and even Wolf showed his excitement, somehow sensing they were nearing home.

Gabe stepped down and walked, Ebony's rein dangling behind him, Wolf beside him, until in the distant darkness, the howl of a lonely wolf penetrated the night. Another howl answered from further on, the cry slowly fading only to be answered by the first. But the first had been joined by another and the two sang in chorus as the eerie howl carried across the flat. Wolf had stopped, listened and soon lifted his voice to the carol of the columbines. Gabe grinned and walked on; the horses used to the cries of Wolf were unconcerned for those that were strangers to them were far away.

Gabe expected Wolf to answer the call of the wild, but he also knew his friend would return. He looked back and saw the shadow disappear among the sage, and whispered, "See you later old friend. Try to stay out of trouble!" He mounted up and with the Grey siding Ebony, they rode through the flat grassy plain. The river bent to the west, meandering through the flats until the long finger ridges stretched out into flat tops and changed the river's course. As the river made the wide bend to the north, the trail Gabe followed cut between the ends of the ridges and mesas to point north. The moon hung high in the sky, making its way west as if the Creator had hung a lantern to light the way.

A coyote tucked its tail as it scampered out of the trail, ducking under a big stand of sage, while a long-eared snowshoe rabbit bounded away. Gabe grinned as he remembered the tale of the rabbit as told by Cougar Woman to the children. *It seems all rabbits had little ears and little feet and the coyotes always caught them and had them for lunch. Until one day the smartest rabbit of them all decided they needed a way to fight back. Now this rabbit had seen the Shoshoni warriors and how they wore the feather of the eagle in their hair to make them look ferocious, so this rabbit asked his friend, the eagle, if he could borrow two of his feathers. The eagle obliged and the rabbit stuck those feathers behind his ears to make them look big. Then he went to his friend the gopher and asked him to help make some big sticks to use on his feet, and he did. The big rabbit attached the sticks to his feet, and hopped away, the sticks helping him to hop very high. Then a coyote came, but when he saw the big ears and big feet, he stopped to stare. That gave the rabbit time to stand really tall and look as big as the coyote. The coyote was afraid and tucked his tail and ran away. So the rabbit asked the Creator to give his family big ears and big feet to keep the coyotes away, and the Creator did just that.* Gabe chuckled at the remembrance, shaking his head at the wisdom of his woman. Then he remembered when Ezra saw his first snowshoe jackrabbit and said it looked, "like a cross between a bunny and a lop-eared mule!" He laughed and lifted his eyes to the mountains, the massive shadows that rode the west edge of the valley, and saw a hint of color on the tips, telling of the approaching sunrise.

The river had come from the deep canyon in the foothills, but the trail pointed to the north and Gabe pointed the horses across the narrow flatlands that edged the many long finger ridges that came from the high Sawatch Mountains. As they crested the long narrow mesa, he could see the white cliffs that stood at the shoulder of the massive granite tipped mountain. The cliffs shown like a white beacon that caught and reflected the moonlight, beckoning Gabe homeward. They dropped off the edge of the long mesa as Gabe glanced to his right to look at the deep shadows of the hills that hid the dark canyon of the river and the place where he and Cougar Woman had met Many Bears and his band of cutthroats. He shook his head at the recollection, always amazed and never surprised at the stubborn stupidity of some people that are blinded by vengeance or greed and so easily misled.

He nudged Ebony to take a slight angle to the left, using the landmark of the white cliffs to guide them. The grey stayed beside them, making Gabe chuckle

that the grey had sided them ever since they heard the
howls of the wolves. He reached out and touched the
grey's neck, "That's alright boy, we understand, don't
we Ebony?" Gabe enjoyed the night, reveling in the
stillness that lay quietly on the valley floor. The shuffling gait of the horses beat a quiet rhythm through
the grasses, in the distance to his right he heard the
argument between a pair of bullfrogs that fought over
the few puddles among the cattails, and in cadence
with the horses, the cicadas rattled their hocks to
give an undercurrent to the soft darkness. He found
a comfort in his solitude, his only companions the
two horses, one that had carried him across the con-
tinent, the other offered his comforting presence to
both man and horse. This was his land, his mountains,
his home, his life. He smiled at the admission, settled
into his saddle and lifted his eyes to the lanterns of the
night, and offered his thanks to his Creator and God.

With the cliffs as the landmark, the flats fell behind
them. The long wrinkle that rolled from the finger
ridge and marked the wide valley almost all the way
to the river dropped them onto the shoulder above
the creek bottomed arroyo that came from the valley
below the cabin. They were nearing home and the
horses seemed to sense that nearness and quickened
their step. Gabe had decided to come from the higher
shoulder that held the upper meadow where the horses grazed. He would strip the horses, hang the gear on

the fence and take the trail through the trees to the cabin. As they came from the trees, the grassy meadow lay before them, but it was empty. Gabe frowned as he looked at the tree line, searching for any horses that might be hidden in the trees, but there were none. He looked at Ebony, his head lifted high, ears forward, nostrils flaring. A glance to the side showed the grey was also alert, looking at the meadow.

Gabe looked back at the trees beside the meadow, turned Ebony to the trail that followed the fence line and take them to the cabin. The grey followed close behind, almost bumping up against Ebony. The trail dropped off the shoulder that held the meadow, cut through the thicker timber, and brought them to the corral behind the cabin. As they neared, the penned horses whinnied, and Ebony let a low whinny rumble in his chest. Gabe looked at the animals in the corral, searching for each one but came up short on the count. He stepped down and stood at the fence, looking them over to see what was missing and saw only one buckskin. Grey Dove's buckskin gelding was there, but the buckskin mare was nowhere to be seen.

Gabe shook his head, wondering what happened and started stripping the gear from the black and the grey. With the saddles and packs in the tack shed, Gabe carried his weapons and saddle bags as he started for the cabin. He was stopped by a voice from the porch, "Bout time!"

Ezra stepped to the edge of the porch, the crutch under his arm, and leaned against the post as he watched Gabe come near. "Glad to see you're in one piece!"

Gabe huffed, and asked, "The buckskin?"

"Grizz."

That was the last thing Gabe wanted to hear.

32 / REUNION

Gabe dropped his gear on the porch and returned to the tack shed to retrieve the parfleche with the bags from the traders. With a broad grin, he dropped the parfleche on the porch and pulled out the big bag of coffee beans and lay it across Ezra's lap as he sat on the rocking chair. Ezra looked at the bag, felt it, and with a broad grin looked up at Gabe. "Where did you find coffee?"

Gabe chuckled, "Some Comancheros, trader from the pueblos down south, came into camp while I was there. Got that," and lifted out the bag of pinole mix, "and this!" He paused, dropped his gaze and mumbled, "Course, I had to kill the trader later."

Ezra frowned, "What's that?"

"Pinole mix. It's a blend of cocoa and spices and more, a popular drink in Mexico, but they use it in breads and such."

"Any good?"

"Of course! And I think the women will like it also."

"Uh, did I hear you right? Did you say you had to kill the trader?" asked Ezra.

"Ummhmm. I had to pay him in gold, and he thought I had more and wanted it. But . . ." and shrugged his shoulders.

"See! I told you that stuff brings trouble! Stone Buffalo thought he was doin' good when he gave us that gold from them Spaniards, but it just brings trouble!"

"I paid him in gold coin and a nugget. You know, the gold I got from the bank when I went to St. Louis."

Ezra shook his head, glanced up at Gabe then back at the bag of coffee beans, "Let's have us a pot o' coffee! We got some thinkin' to do!" He struggled to his feet, looked at Gabe, "Grind us up some o' them beans, I'll put on a pot o' water!"

The aroma from the fresh ground beans wafted up as Gabe ground the handful of beans on the broad flat rock at the edge of the clearing. He added a few more to the pile and used the smaller rock to grind away. A soft hand touched his shoulder and the familiar voice said, "My man has returned."

Cougar Woman bent down to embrace him, but he stood and turned to take her in his arms and give a lingering embrace. They kissed and leaned back to look at one another, "Do we have peace with the Comanche?"

"Old Owl and White Knife convinced the council, and we have peace," he stated, smiling at his beautiful woman. "But . . ."

"But?"

"Many Bears tried again, and I had to kill him," he dropped his eyes as he spoke, "he led a small band and a Comanchero trader to my camp. I expected them and Wolf and I did what we needed, and I'm hopin' it's all over."

Cougar frowned, looked around, "Where *is* Wolf?"

Gabe grinned, "Oh, he heard the lonesome cry of some female or females and decided to pay 'em a visit. He'll probably be back soon."

Cougar smiled and laughed, "Your breakfast will be ready soon. The boys will be excited to see you." She handed him a cup for the ground coffee and with cup in hand started back to the cabin. Gabe stood, stretched, and smiled as he looked over the clearing, the cabin, and the corrals beyond. He walked back to the cabin, climbed the porch steps, and went inside to join his family.

A short while later, the men were seated on the porch, steaming coffee cups in hand, as Gabe asked, "So, what about this Grizz?"

Ezra shook his head, slapped the crutch that lay beside him, "It was two nights ago. I thought I heard somethin' and crawled outta bed to go see. When I stood on the porch, I heard the ruckus, the horses screamin', the bear roarin' and such, but I couldn't do nothin'!" He growled and slapped at his leg, "We found the buckskin in the mornin' after I hobbled up the trail. So we brought the rest of 'em down here. I don't think he came back, but . . ." he let the remark trail off as he grumbled something about feeling useless.

"Well, we'll just hafta go up there and look at things. If there's much of a carcass left, he'll probably come back, but if not, he'll prob'ly wait till he gets hungry again and *then* come back. He'll prob'ly be thinkin' it was pretty easy huntin' for him, what with the horses all penned up and couldn't get away," surmised Gabe.

"Yeah, prob'ly. But do we go after him?" asked Ezra.

"We?"

"Yeah, we! I don't care if I gotta hobble all the way on this stick, I'm goin'!" he growled.

"As cranky as he's been lately, he'll probably want to take on that grizzly with his crutch!" declared Grey Dove as she came through the doorway, Cougar Woman close behind. The little ones had already bounced off the porch and were playing in the clearing as the men watched.

"And I wouldn't want to be the bear he goes after!" added Cougar, chuckling as she sat on the bench beside her man.

Gabe looked at Dove, "And you're willing to let your man go grizzly huntin' with a broken leg and all?"

Dove laughed, "What's the worst that could happen. Either he'll kill the bear, or the bear will eat him! Either way, at least I won't have to listen to his moaning and groaning and complaining anymore!" and giggled, looking at her man with a mischievous grin.

"Now that's a fine how do you do!" He looked at Gabe, "You go runnin' off to play paddy cake with the Comanche, I stay home and protect the women and now she wants to feed me to the bears! I never!" he grumbled as he crossed his arms on his chest and did his best to look indignant. Dove laughed, and came to his side and started tickling him, knowing he was the most ticklish person she knew, and within moments, both were laughing and rollicking as he tried to make her stop.

When the laughter subsided, a serious tone settled on the porch and Gabe asked, "Are you serious about coming with me?" "You bet I am! I'm tired of sittin' around and feelin' helpless. I'll be able to ride alright, it's just the gettin' on that's the problem. You help me on, I'll be fine."

"What about gettin' off?"

Ezra chuckled, "I can always fall off!"

Gabe bent down, put his shoulder under Ezra's rump and lifted him up beside his bay. Ezra swung his leg over the pommel of the saddle, scooted onto the seat, stuffed his toes in the stirrups and nodded,

"I'm ready!"

Gabe swung aboard Ebony and started to the trail to go to the upper meadow. As they neared the fence, Ezra said, "The carcass was over in that corner," pointing to the near lower corner to their right.

"Then let's stay along the fence till we get there. No sense goin' in and havin' to come back out to track him down."

One magpie was hopping around the debris covered carcass, a badger scampered away as the men rode up. Gabe leaned closer to the fence and saw the remains had been covered by dirt, clumps of grass, leaves and sticks, everything that had been in the near vicinity had been clawed up and used to cover the carcass. It was a typical practice of the big bruins, having eaten their fill, they would hide their kill so they could return and finish gorging themselves on the left-overs.

Gabe looked at Ezra, "Looks to me like he's plannin' on returnin'."

"But when? There's no way of tellin'. Could be tonight, tomorrow, anytime."

"Then maybe we better go lookin' for him. He's prob'ly holed up somewhere takin' a snooze with his fat belly and all."

"We need Wolf to track him down," observed Ezra, looking around as if expecting to see the black wolf suddenly appear.

"Yeah, but we can't wait on him. He's on one of his love rendezvous and could be gone a week or more." He chuckled as he nudged Ebony toward the corner of the fence where it appeared the bear had come through. With a wave to Ezra, Gabe pushed on, trailing the big bear. The paw prints twice the size of Gabe's hand and more, the claws dug into the dirt about four inches in front of the paw print, both telling Gabe this was a big bear. He frowned as he remembered the big grizzly he saw at the upper end of the gorge when he took the elk and big horn sheep before going to the Comanche camp. *Maybe it's the same one. It's not common for two big boars to be in the same territory so it probably is the same one.*

The horses moved quietly on the pine needle laden trail that twisted among the trees. The trail was on the shoulder of the slope that flanked the mountains on the south side of the big gorge. The bear sign showed the beast was in no hurry, moving at an ambling walk, the prints staggered as they would with a walking pace. If the bear was running or in a charge, his prints would show the leap-frog type movements with front paws together, hind paws coming forward on either side, and repeated. When the sign left the trail, Gabe reined up and stood in his stirrups to look around, hesitant to go into the thicker timber where there was little room to maneuver and escape. He saw a talus slope beside a sheer cliff face, towering walls of limestone topped by a cluster of scraggly juniper and turned to Ezra. "Looks like a good place for a cave or a den, might need to check it out."

"You mean, *you* might need to check it out. I ain't gettin' off this horse less'n I absolutely have to!"

Gabe shrugged, slipped the Ferguson from the scabbard, checked the load in both the rifle and his belt pistol, then on second thought swapped the belt pistol for one of the saddle pistols. He stepped down and handed the reins to Ezra, and walked into the thicket of aspen, following the sign of the bear.

33 / GRIZZLY

The thick stand of aspen was populated with saplings, most about the thickness of a man's forearm and so close together Gabe often had to slip sideways between the white barked trees. The bigger trees at the upper end of the stand gave way as the deep layer of matted cast-off leaves showed sign of the long claws of the grizzly digging deep as the big bruin assaulted the steep slope. A solitary ponderosa masked Gabe's approach to the talus and the overhang and Gabe paused beside the red barked giant and smelled bear. A quick glance at the bark showed tufts of hair telling Gabe the bear had used this as a back scratcher, but the strong smell also told of the bear marking his territory.

Gabe slowly shook his head, searching through the few trees at the foot of the talus and cliff face, but seeing nothing. He stepped away from the ponderosa, watching every footfall on the precarious rock-strewn slope. A stone slipped, and he fell to one knee, catching himself with his free hand. The rock clattered down below, bouncing from stone to stone, alerting every creature within hearing. Gabe paused, stood erect, a stabbing pain in his knee making him wince, and he thought he saw movement. The lichen and moss-covered limestone showed green, orange, brown, and every shade of grey and black, but nothing stirred. He smelled bear but was uncertain if it was the beast or the territory markings. The stone offered uncertain footing, but he knew he had to make it to the slight shoulder before the cliff face; that flat ledge would be the perfect lair for the bear.

He paused to catch his breath and strengthen his resolve, then started his ascent again, watching every step as he moved from rock to rock. He glanced from the edge of the shoulder above him to the rocks below, but the huff and snort from above him made him stop and slowly turn to look up. The massive head of the grizzly was moving side to side, nostrils flaring, teeth showing and mouth dripping saliva. Gabe knew the eyesight of the big bruin was poor, but his sense of smell was excellent. Gabe's stained buckskins gave a little camouflage, but the big bear rose on his hind legs, towering above the ledge and dwarfing the nearby stones and scraggly juniper.

The bear cocked his head to the side, then sounded

off with a roar that seemed to make even the rocks tremble. The sound filled the canyon, aspen leaves fluttered to show their grey undersides, birds took flight, and Gabe spun around to face the monster, bringing the Ferguson to full cock and he brought it in line with the massive chest. Without hesitation, he dropped the hammer and the big rifle bucked, rocking Gabe back on his heels on the precarious footing. The big ball impacted the beast's chest, dust puffed, and the bear flinched, slapped at his chest as if a pesky bug had dared to strike. The bear roared his anger, took two clumsy steps forward and lowered his head between his shoulders to glare downslope at the intruder to his domain.

Gabe frantically spun the trigger guard to open the breech, stuffed a patched ball into the opening, jerked the plug on the powder horn with his teeth and poured black powder in the breech. Spinning the trigger guard to close the breech, he flipped up the frizzen, poured powder in the pan and slapped the frizzen closed. He looked up as he eared back the hammer and saw the beast drop to all fours. Gabe lifted the Ferguson, took a quick sight just below the jaw of the beast and fired. Again the Ferguson roared, bucked, and spat lead. The bullet disappeared under the jaw of the beast, and Gabe was not certain he scored a hit. But the bear was angered and lunged off the ledge. This was his territory, and he was incensed, he bounded from flat rock to flat rock, never taking his eyes off his quarry.

Gabe snatched the big saddle pistol from his belt and eared back both hammers. He leveled the weapon at the bear, steadying his grip with his other hand, his only target the colossal head of the mountain monster and pulled both triggers. The pistol blasted, the roar of the twin explosions echoing across the canyon behind them, and the bear flinched as one of the lead balls plowed a furrow across the top of his skull. But still he came; mouth agape, teeth bared, slobber flying over his shoulder, bounding from stone to stone.

Gabe spun on his heels, looked downslope and stretched out his long legs to jump from stone to stone, moving like a ballet dancer on a private stage, the only accompaniment the roaring of his nemesis in brown. Gabe hit the ponderosa with his shoulder and twisted behind it, glancing over his shoulder and the bear, less than fifteen feet behind. But the beast hit a flat slide rock that teetered on uncertain balance and the bear slipped, dropped to his shoulder but quickly rose again. The bewildered grizzly paused, looking for his prey, but Gabe was behind the big ponderosa, quietly and quickly reloading the rifle.

The bear rose to his full height on his hind legs, pawing the air with his forelegs, and roared, his big mouth wide enough to swallow a boulder, or Gabe's head, whichever came first. Without a clear shot, Gabe leaned the rifle against the trunk of the ponderosa and started to reload both barrels of the saddle pistol, but the bear dropped to all fours and started into the aspen grove.

Gabe shook his head, realizing the beast apparently caught the scent of the horses and man, and was bound for another quarry. Gabe jammed the loaded pistol in his belt, snatched up the Ferguson and started after the beast. He was amazed to see the tops of the aspen part like waves on a lake, as the monstrous grizzly pushed his way through. Gabe shouted, hoping Ezra could hear, "He's coming! The Grizz is coming!"

The shout made the bear stop and turn to look back, but the strong scent of horse and man was more enticing, and he lunged through the rest of the aspen, coming face to face with the horses. Ebony reared up, pawing at the air, cocking his head to the side as he whinnied a scream of warning to the monster. Ezra was fighting to stay aboard the panicked bay that was side-stepping, his ears forward, nostrils flaring, wide eyed and trying to get away. Ezra sat firm in his saddle, gripping the panicked horse with his legs, holding his Lancaster rifle across his legs and the pommel with a death grip, turning and craning his neck for a look at the charging bear.

The bear feinted a charge at the black stallion, but Ebony lunged at the beast, teeth bared and kicked at the monster with his forelegs. He spun around, took aim over his shoulder, and kicked the bear in the face and neck. The beast stumbled back, turned toward the other horse, and started a charge. The bay reared up, twisted, and unseated Ezra who plummeted to the ground, hitting flat of his back, and knocking the wind from his lungs, but he held the rifle tight. He tried to suck air, struggled, and twisted to see where the big bruin was and saw the monster charging. Big eyes filled with hate and a lust for blood glared at Ezra, a roar came from the mouth that showed teeth big enough to bite through a log, and a tongue that thirsted for fresh meat. Ezra rolled to face the charge, brought the long-barreled Lancaster up one handed and eared back the hammer, pulled the trigger, and obscured the beast with a cloud of blue/grey smoke. The roar of the rifle and the beast were discordant, and the bear stumbled and fell on his right shoulder. Ezra squirmed out of reach, came to his feet, and turned to face the bear as he rose to all fours. Ezra felt at his belt for the pistol, but it was gone.

A blast from the edge of the trees sent another .62 caliber ball driving into the chest of the beast, making the bear stumble to the side like a drunken sailor on a narrow wharf. Gabe walked forward, his pistol held before him, and as he neared the monster, the bear turned to face him. The brown behemoth's jaw dropped open and he cocked his head to roar but swallowed two lead balls when Gabe dropped both hammers on the pistol. The only roar heard was the blast from the twin barreled pistol.

The grizzly, a silver-tip male, fell back and crumpled to the ground. His enormous head hit the ground with a thud, but the mouth was open, eyes stared sightless, and his last breath wheezed through the bullet destroyed gullet.

Gabe looked at the bear, then to Ezra, "I see you got off your horse alright."

Ezra huffed as he stood with his weight on his good leg, using his rifle as a crutch, and looked at his friend then at the bear. "Well, at least we won't have to carry him far."

"Nope. But how we gonna get him back?"

They wasted little time skinning the bear and preparing the bundle of meat and hide for transport, but the stench of bear causes any horse to be a little more than skittish and more often downright disagreeable. But they put the bundle aboard Ebony and Gabe walked, leading, and reassuring the horse all the way as they trailed after Ezra aboard his bay. When they came into the clearing at the cabin, Gabe quickly dropped the bundle near the tree line and led a still nervous Ebony to the corral. He helped Ezra to dismount, then stripped the horses of the tack and hung it on the fence, but the smell of bear on Gabe's saddle was spooking the horses, so he carried it back to the porch.

The women waited on the porch, the children were inside napping, and Cougar Woman stood as Gabe came near. As she pinched her nose, "Whoooeee! You smell like bear! You two stay right there, we'll get you some clothes and blankets and you can get rid of that smell in the creek down below!"

Gabe looked at Ezra, "You know, a dip in one of those hot springs would feel good!"

34 / VISITORS

The hide had been rinsed in the hot water of the spring and was now staked out at the edge of the clearing. Cougar and Dove had scraped it, stretched it, and staked it out ready for the application of the brain slurry, but now they sat with Gabe and Ezra on the porch, enjoying the time together. The men had cups of steaming coffee, the women had come to like the pinole and were sipping at cups of the spicy brew. While the women had worked on the hide, Gabe and Ezra repaired the fence at the corner of the meadow, buried the rest of the horse carcass, and taken all the horses to the meadow for the deep grasses and fresh water from the spring fed creek. It had been a busy day and they were enjoying the time of relaxing on the porch.

A glimpse of black in the trees caught Gabe's attention as he started to rise, but the familiar figure of a big black wolf trotted into the clearing, tongue lolling to the side, his head held high and a definite smile on his face as he casually climbed the steps to the porch and lay his head on Cougar's lap, looking up at her with big eyes that rolled to look at Gabe sitting close beside his woman. Gabe reached over to pet the wolf's head, chuckling, "Well, if you don't look like you're as happy as can be, you musta really enjoyed your little interlude with the ladies!"

Cougar cradled his face in her palms, lifted it and looked in his eyes, "Do not listen to him, Wolf. You are a good boy and I'm glad you're home." He appeared to be enjoying the attention, his tail wagging as he excitedly pranced about, until he suddenly turned to face the clearing, standing at the head of the steps. He stood rigid, head up, ears standing tall, the stance of alertness but not alarm. He stared at the trail, and the sound of approaching horses filtered through the trees. Wolf bounded off the steps to stand before the cabin, assuming an attack stance as he let a low growl come from deep in his chest.

Gabe reached for his Ferguson rifle that stood beside the door, Ezra lifted the Lancaster from beside him, and Cougar and Dove hustled the children into the cabin. With a glance to Ezra, Gabe left the porch with two long strides and went to the trees while Ezra stood to lean against the porch post and lifted his rifle to his shoulder. Wolf took two cautious steps forward, watching the trail, nose in the air, and a glance toward Gabe, now hidden in the trees. Wolf cut and ran to Gabe, leaving Ezra to guard the cabin.

"*Haa marúawe! Hello!*" The greeting was in the tongue of the Comanche and Gabe recognized the voice.

As Gabe stepped from the trees, he saw White Knife, his young son riding behind him, followed by Little Rabbit. Both were leading horses. A broad smile painted White Knife's face as they came into the clearing and Gabe stepped close to extend his hand to welcome his friend. "Step down, step down! It is good to see you," and he looked to Little Rabbit, "And you too, Little Rabbit."

White Knife handed Gabe the lead line to one horse, slipped down and reached up to help his son to the ground. He took the lead line from Little Rabbit and helped her to the ground. Cougar Woman had come from the cabin and greeted the visitors warmly, quickly leading Little Rabbit, with her son's hand held tightly, to the cabin to meet Grey Dove and the children.

"It is good to see you, my friend," began Gabe as the men walked to the corral to put the horses away. "These are some fine-looking horses White Knife, I especially like that line-back dun, she's a well-built animal. But why are you with two horses? Taking a long journey, are you?"

White Knife grinned, looked at Gabe and glanced

to Ezra who was negotiating well on his rapidly healing leg with the help of a walking stick. "These are for
you. Old Owl and the others of the council wanted to
let you know they are still committed to peace even
after Many Bears' shameful attack."

"That was not necessary. I knew Many Bears acted
on his own, but these," nodding to the horses, "are
more than deserved. What can I do to repay such a
fine gift?"

White Knife grinned, "While you were with us, my
father admired your big stallion. He would like a colt
from that big black." He chuckled, "As you can tell,
these are both mares," nodding to the gift horses, "and
they are coming into their time. If they are bred soon,
the colts will come in early summer, a good time to
visit our people."

"Oh, I get it. That wily old fox had that in mind all
the time, didn't he?" chuckled Gabe, glancing from
White Knife to the horses.

Ezra leaned against the fence, his forearms resting
on the top rail, "That blood sorrel is mighty purty
with those white stockings and that blaze face, she *is*
purty!" Gabe readily agreed, admiring both animals.

Gabe turned from the corral and started to the cabin, the others walking alongside. He glanced at White
Knife, "The mares will be a welcome addition to our
herd. We lost one of our mares while I was visiting
your village, a big grizzly decided he wanted some

horsemeat and took down a nice buckskin mare."

"Is that what you have staked out there?" asked White Knife, nodding to the hide at the edge of the clearing.

"That's him," answered Gabe. White Knife started toward the hide for a looksee and went to one knee to examine the fur. The hide stretched almost ten-foot square and White Knife stepped off the length and width. He saw the silver-tip fur at the edge of the hide, looked up at Gabe, "He was a big bear, and old too."

"He looked a lot bigger when he was charging," declared Ezra, laughing.

The men walked to the porch and White Knife saw the grizzly claws drying on the porch railing, picked one up and lay it in his palm. The claw was almost as long as the width of White Knife's out-stretched palm and he shook his head in amazement. "I have never killed a great bear," shaking his head. The men knew that among the plains Indians, the killing of a great bear was considered an exceptional feat of bravery and held all in high esteem that wore a necklace of the bear's claws. He glanced to Gabe, "This is not your first, you wore a claw necklace when you visited my people."

Gabe nodded, "Ummhmmm. We've managed to run into a few o' them big bears as we travel the mountains." He nodded to Ezra, "Black Buffalo there has one o' them necklaces too."

White Knife looked from Gabe to Ezra as he replaced the claw, "Spirit Bear says that you are a great warrior and have killed many of your enemies."

Ezra frowned, looked at Gabe with a questioning look and back to White Knife, "We don't go lookin' for fights, White Knife, but it seems like there's plenty of folks out there that just don't seem to mind gettin' us into *their* fights. I'd just as soon never kill another man or beast, but sometimes we just gotta do what we gotta do!" White Knife frowned, mentally sorting out what Ezra said, then nodded his agreement.

It was two days later when the new friends mounted up to return to their home in the valley of the Arkansa. White Knife reached down to clasp forearms with Gabe, "I see you as my brother, Spirit Bear. You and your family will always be welcome in our village." He looked up to Ezra, "And you as well, Black Buffalo. I hope you all will join us for the buffalo hunt when the season of colors comes."

"We'll certainly give it a try, White Knife. If we don't see you before then, let Old Owl know the mares will probably foal after the green-up. Perhaps you could bring him with you!" suggested Gabe.

White Knife grinned, "If he comes, he will probably bring another mare for your stallion."

Both men laughed as Gabe stepped back. As they rode from the clearing, both White Knife and Little Rabbit turned to wave as they dropped into the trees and out of sight. Cougar stood beside Gabe, "She is a good woman. I like her."

Gabe grinned, pulled Cougar close, "It's good to have new friends. Perhaps we'll visit them come fall, maybe for that buffalo hunt."

Ezra looked at Gabe, "If we go after buffalo again, I'll find me a big tree and stay outta the way of any o' them big bulls!"

The others laughed, remembering the dreadful injuries Ezra suffered in the last buffalo hunt and the long-time of healing for the man. In the past, Gabe had a run-in with buffalo also, but both men knew it was the way of the land. With great risk comes great reward and in their minds, there was no greater reward than to have a fantastic life with a wonderful family in the middle of the magnificence of God's creation.

They walked back to the cabin, couples' arm in arm, laughed at the children playing with Wolf, and went to the porch and their familiar rocking chairs. Cougar called the little ones to come to the cabin and Chipmunk and Bobcat ushered the little ones to the porch. Gabe frowned when he saw Wolf pause and look back to the trees, then a spot of grey caught his eye. Gabe nudged Cougar, pointed to the trees with his chin, and they watched Wolf trot to the tree line and greet a grey wolf with a proud stance as she cowered before him, tail tucked, and began licking his face. She came alongside him, as they both looked to the cabin. Gabe spoke softly to Cougar, "Looks like there's gonna be some black wolf pups soon."

Cougar giggled, "Don't you think we have enough little ones already?"

Gabe frowned and looked at his grinning wife, then leaned over to kiss his sweetheart.

WATCH FOR APACHE AMBUSH, THE NEXT
NOVEL IN THE STONECROFT SAGA

COMING SOON

ABOUT THE AUTHOR

Born and raised in Colorado into a family of ranchers and cow-boys, B.N. Rundell is the youngest of seven sons. Juggling bull riding, skiing, and high school, graduation was a launching pad for a hitch in the Army Paratroopers. After the army, he finished his college education in Springfield, MO, and together with his wife and growing family, entered the ministry as a Baptist preacher.

Together, B.N. and Dawn raised four girls that are now married and have made them proud grandparents. With many years as a successful pastor and educator, he retired from the ministry and followed in the footsteps of his entre-preneurial father and started a successful insurance agency, which is now in the hands of his trusted nephew. He has also been a successful audiobook narrator and has recorded many books for several award-winning authors. Now finally realizing his life-long dream, B.N. has turned his efforts to writing a variety of books, from children's picture books and young adult adventure books, to the historical fiction and western genres.